"Why, exactly, *did* you make such a ridiculous bid?

I don't know who you are, but I can't imagine you have any problem meeting men or finding dates."

"What makes you say that?"

"Look at you." Roman's gaze connected with hers and it felt a bit like she could see right through him. "You're beautiful."

"Thank you, but I don't need you to say things like that to me, okay?"

"Okay..."

"I paid quite a lot for a sliver of time with you, and I intend to get my money's worth."

"What does that mean, exactly?"

She turned to him and extended her hand. "My name is Taylor Klein and I have spent the last several weeks trying to get to you. I need you for your brain. And your creativity."

"So you don't want to go out to dinner with me?"

She sat back in her seat. "Not particularly. Especially not if you're thinking about wine and candles and all of that."

Roman couldn't have been more confused—or intrigued—if he tried. This exquisite woman didn't want even a little romance? She only wanted his mind? "Okay, then. Tell me more."

* * *

Black Tie Bachelor Bid by Karen Booth is part of the Little Black Book of Secrets series.

Dear Reader,

Yay! It's time to roll out book two in the Little Black Book of Secrets trilogy. This sexy series centers on childhood best friends Chloe, Taylor and Alexandra, and an anonymous social media account exposing the secrets and scandals of old-money families like their own. It's all quite juicy...

The bachelor is Roman Scott, a mysterious and reclusive hotelier. Roman is also a widower and has shut himself off from women, but when his sister-in-law organizes a charity bachelor auction, he reluctantly says yes. That brings in determined Taylor, our heroine, who has failed at every career she's pursued. Her latest idea is converting her family's summer estate in Connecticut into a boutique hotel. But she needs the advice of a brilliant innovator like Roman. So she bids a wild amount and wins him. When they steal away to Connecticut, it's passion like neither expected—and intrigue as they try to unmask Little Black Book.

I hope you have as much fun reading this book as I did writing it! Drop me a line at karen@karenbooth.net and let me know your thoughts!

Karen

KAREN BOOTH

—

BLACK TIE BACHELOR BID

HARLEQUIN
DESIRE

Recycling programs
for this product may
not exist in your area.

ISBN-13: 978-1-335-73562-1

Black Tie Bachelor Bid

Copyright © 2022 by Karen Booth

For questions and comments about the quality of this book,
please contact us at CustomerService@Harlequin.com.

Harlequin Enterprises ULC
22 Adelaide St. West, 41st Floor
Toronto, Ontario M5H 4E3, Canada
www.Harlequin.com

Printed in U.S.A.

Karen Booth is a Midwestern girl transplanted in the South, raised on '80s music and repeated readings of *Forever...* by Judy Blume. When she takes a break from the art of romance, she's listening to music with her college-age kids or sweet-talking her husband into making her a cocktail. Learn more about Karen at karenbooth.net.

Books by Karen Booth

Harlequin Desire

Blue Collar Billionaire

Little Black Book of Secrets

The Problem with Playboys
Black Tie Bachelor Bid

The Sterling Wives

Once Forbidden, Twice Tempted
High Society Secrets
All He Wants for Christmas

Visit her Author Profile page at Harlequin.com, or karenbooth.net, for more titles.

You can also find Karen Booth on Facebook, along with other Harlequin Desire authors, at Facebook.com/harlequindesireauthors!

One

"No way. It's too sexy." Taylor Klein shook her head, dismissing the slinky low-cut black dress her friend Alexandra Gold was holding on a hanger. Along with Chloe Burnett, the three best friends were sifting through the most elegant contents of the expansive closet in Taylor's Manhattan apartment, searching for a suitable gown for the high-dollar bachelor auction Taylor was set to attend that evening.

"Why would you not want to be sexy?" Chloe flipped her sumptuous red tresses over her shoulder, a sure sign that she was exasperated.

"Because I want to be professional." Taylor zipped past more dresses. *Nope... Nope... Nope...* None of them were right. Or at least she didn't feel like she could pull any of them off. Yes, these were her clothes, but her already shaky confidence had been worn down to a fraction of what it had once been. There was a lot on the line with this auction. She had to look perfect.

"You're about to pay money for a date with a handsome billionaire." Chloe threw up her hands, giving up on the search and instead perching on the tufted white velvet ottoman at the center of the closet. "I'd say that any hopes of professional have sailed a long time ago."

Said handsome billionaire, Roman Scott, was one of the most innovative and successful hoteliers in the world. He took old buildings and gave them all-new lives as chic and ultracool lodgings. "My attempts at approaching him in a businesslike manner didn't work. So now I have to go to a bachelor auction instead." Taylor could hardly believe this was her lot in life, but she was determined to make it work. After years of failed career starts, she had an idea for a new venture—turning her family's summertime estate in Connecticut into a boutique hotel. It would play to Taylor's strengths—a flair for design, an endless need to make others happy and a great attention to detail. Taylor also believed in extensive preparation, and that meant getting the very best advice before jumping into the deep end on a multimillion-dollar venture. As far as she was concerned, the best advice would only come from Roman Scott. Only him. No one else.

"I still can't believe he didn't call you back. I

would be so mad. And insulted." Alexandra, or Alex as they all called her, was a highly sought high-end floral designer, softhearted and optimistic to a fault. It took a lot to make her express any negative emotion.

"How many messages did you leave for him? And did you make sure he knew that you're a Klein? Your family is an institution, especially in the Northeast. He's from this part of the country. There's no way he doesn't know who you or your family are." This was a predictable reaction from Chloe, who owned a crisis PR firm. She was always looking for connections, in part because she had a knack at leveraging them.

Nothing about this discussion was helping with Taylor's confidence. "I left more than a dozen phone messages for him, plus I sent several emails, and I even tried a fax if you can believe that. Nothing worked. The guy would not call me."

"Maybe he's a jerk," Chloe said. "Isn't that what he's known for?"

"Yes. In some circles," Taylor said. Indeed, Roman Scott had a reputation for being moody and elusive. But Taylor knew that the most disagreeable people were often the most talented. Add in Roman's good looks and it made the prospect of meeting him even more daunting, but Taylor needed to accept the fact that very little in this situation was in her control. "It doesn't matter. I want this to work. I want to find something I'm good at. I *need* to find something I'm good at. I think Roman Scott can help me. So I have to try. Even if he's a jerk."

Alex reached for Taylor's arm. "Can I be honest?"

"Always." The three women had been close friends since they were in seventh grade and met at the elite Baldwell School for Girls in central Connecticut. They each came from great wealth and power, but that could mean a chaotic existence, however privileged it might be. Friendship kept them grounded. They'd been a safe harbor for each other through countless ups and downs, including Chloe's nonstop drama with her mom, Alex's canceled million-dollar wedding and Taylor's endless string of bad breakups. The three friends could tell each other anything. *Anything.*

"You're trying to impress a very powerful but enigmatic man. He has seen the world one hundred times over and probably been with countless women. You'll want to stand out. And that means you have to dress sexy."

Taylor sighed. She knew Alex and Chloe were right. They simply hadn't taken into account Taylor's bigger problem—*men* plus *sexy* were a disastrous equation for her. She'd had her heart broken more times than she could count. It was so bad that her New Year's resolution had been zero tolerance for romance. Love and men were off the table, and she'd done great with sticking to it so far. It was already May and she'd not only kept her promise, she was on a much more even keel. She didn't want to stop now. Plus, a meeting with Roman Scott would be easier if she was sure he didn't see her as a woman or a sexual being. But maybe it was time to admit that she needed to set aside her personal goals in favor of the professional. She wanted to get this hotel project off the ground. She needed Mr. Scott's help, but she also needed his attention. "Fine. Tell me what you'd wear if you were me."

That got Chloe off the ottoman. She sprang to her feet and beelined for the black slinky gown she'd suggested minutes earlier. "This one. It's a slam dunk."

Taylor's stomach lurched just thinking about the horrible night she'd last worn that very expensive garment. "I got dumped in that dress. I should have burned it."

"Dumped by whom?" Chloe asked, incredulous.

"Ian."

"Oh, right. Well, Ian isn't smart enough to know how amazing you are. I bet you looked smoking hot in this."

"I did. It still didn't change the fact that he'd met someone else."

Alex plucked the dress from Chloe's hand, marched it to the other side of the closet and hung it up in a section near the door. "That needs to be donated. Immediately." She turned and made her way back to a different gown. "What about this one? It's gorgeous. Impeccably made. And it still has the tags on it, so hopefully there's nothing bad associated with it." Alex pulled out the hanger and presented her find—pale gold and strapless, with a fitted bodice and fine metallic threads woven into the full and gauzy skirt.

"Honestly, I forgot I had it. I bought it on a lark. It was on sale and I just thought it was too pretty to leave in the store." Taylor stepped closer and took the fabric in her hand. It had a beautiful drape and it sparkled in the light. Most important, she remembered how well it showed off her not-quite-ample bust. "I can live with this."

Chloe plucked a pair of strappy gold heels from the shoe section. "These will go perfectly."

"Okay, then. I guess I have a dress."

"Thank God," Chloe said. "Now let's get you into it."

Chloe and Alex helped Taylor get dressed, then went to work picking out accessories. They kept it simple and timeless—gold and diamonds, a necklace and matching earrings that had once belonged to her beloved grandmother. Taylor stood before the full-length mirror in her closet, while Chloe and Alex looked on. She felt confident in this dress, but even that made her second-guess herself. She'd felt sure of lots of things in the past—career choices and men, and she'd always been proven wrong.

"I have a good feeling about tonight," Alex said. "Roman Scott is going to be blown away by your beauty."

"*And* your business idea," Chloe added.

Taylor's shoulders tightened. "I'm far more worried about the latter."

"You sure you don't want either of us to come with you?" Alex asked.

"I can't. I have plans with Parker." Chloe pulled her phone out of her bag and consulted it, surely looking for a text from her fiancé, Parker Sullivan.

Taylor and Alex exchanged knowing glances. For two people who swore they didn't believe in love or commitment, Chloe and Parker were inseparable and completely head over heels. Alex was holding out hope to find the same for herself someday, but Taylor was mostly convinced she'd already used up her chances at love. "Something romantic?" Taylor asked.

"No," Chloe said. "We're having dinner at our place with Parker's investigator, Jessica. He's got her looking into Little Black Book. He won't back off. He's obsessed with stopping them. He says they're pure evil."

Little Black Book was an anonymous social media account with millions of followers. It specialized in unveiling the scandalous secrets of rich and powerful people. At first, it had seemed as though Little Black Book's approach was scattershot, but a pattern was developing, one that was quite scary for Taylor, Alex and Chloe. Thus far, every person targeted had a tie to either their alma mater, the Baldwell School for Girls or Sedgefield Academy, a boys preparatory school a few miles from Baldwell. Parker and Chloe's mom had been the first to notice the connection.

"I can't say I disagree," Alex said.

"It's gossip. People can't let it bother them so

much. You just give the situation more oxygen, and the world always moves on to something new. Always," Taylor said.

"No. You're wrong. Gossip can destroy people's lives." The corners of Alex's mouth turned down in a frown.

Taylor realized how insensitive she'd just been. Alex had been dragged by the tabloids for weeks after she canceled her wedding, which had been dubbed the "society event of the year." Taylor wasn't about to mention the fact that Alex had survived all of it and was doing well now. "You're right. I'm sorry."

"Well, regardless, I should probably run," Chloe said. "Parker hates it when I'm late."

"It's okay. Thanks for offering to come with me tonight, Alex, but I need to do this on my own," Taylor said. "I hope you both know how much I appreciate your help and support. I love you." She gave each of her friends a big hug.

"We love you, too," Chloe said.

"Always," Alex said, then she and Chloe headed for the door. "Good luck. We know you can do it."

"Thanks. I'll let you know what happens." Taylor grabbed a few essentials, chucked them into a matching evening bag and made her way downstairs to meet her driver. As she rode through the night, she ignored her nervousness. Roman Scott was just a man. She was going to bid on him for charity, win the auction no matter the price, and then she would mine him for information. This was not a complicated plan, even if it did feel a bit unconventional. She could do this. For herself.

When she arrived at the hotel where the auction was taking place, she didn't dawdle. She rode up the escalator to the second-floor ballroom, collected her auction paddle and took a seat in the front row. The room was abuzz with activity, slowly filling up with wealthy and powerful people, most of whom were women.

Taylor was laser focused as the emcee, a woman named Fiona Scott, walked out onto the stage and the spotlight shined on her. Taylor, always thorough with her due diligence, had learned that Fiona was Roman's sister-in-law, and married to Roman's older brother, Derrick. The couple were clearly expecting a child soon. If Taylor had to guess, she would've put Fiona at around seven months pregnant. "Ladies, I'm so glad you're here to support my foundation, which raises money for several rare diseases," Fiona said. "I promise that you will not be disappointed with what we have to offer this evening, a truly stunning lineup of the most generous men you could imagine. Now, before we start the bidding, I'd like to whet your appetite for what's to come. Gentlemen, can you please come on out?"

The velvet curtain parted at the far end of the stage, and one by one, good-looking men in tuxedos filed onto the stage. The audience members stood, and quiet clapping gave way for more enthusiastic applause as countless flashbulbs from the press in attendance threatened to blind them all. Many of the bachelors responded with a flirtatious smile or a friendly wave. A few punctuated it all with a wink. Some delivered smoldering stares. All were men Taylor knew of—Hollywood actors, Wall Street bigwigs and real estate moguls. There were even a few male models thrown into the mix, which came as no huge surprise since the opening bid this evening was the considerable sum of $25,000. Fiona Scott intended to raise a lot of money.

Taylor's heart picked up when she spotted her intended target, Roman. She stood a little straighter as he strode across the stage. He was much taller in person than she'd pictured, even though she knew him to be six-three. Somehow he was far more handsome than any photograph she'd seen, as if no camera could fully capture the magic of his square jaw, straight nose and inquisitive eyebrows. His thick dark hair was a touchable mop, with a hint of sexy salt-and-pepper. Even from a distance, his eyes were the deepest blue she could imagine, leaving her with far more questions than answers. Roman was a lot to take in. A delicious mix of masculinity and mystery she hoped was the key to her future.

Just as quickly as he'd walked across the stage, he disappeared behind the black velvet curtain. Taylor slowly dropped to her seat, noticing how short her breaths had become and the way her chest was heaving. Part of her couldn't wait for the moment when she won her auction and could get Roman Scott alone. Another part of her was absolutely terrified.

Roman Scott, in the flesh, was so much more enticing than she'd thought possible.

Humiliating didn't begin to describe what Roman Scott was feeling as he walked backstage and tracked down his brother, Derrick. "Will you remind me to never, ever do you or your wife another favor?" Roman tugged at the bow tie that was currently strangling him. He'd worn black-tie clothing to thousands of events, but something about this particular tux on this particular night was making him feel as though he was being choked alive.

"Get over yourself. It's for a good cause." Derrick took a sip of bourbon. It was easy for him to dismiss the high-dollar charity bachelor auction as simply being for a good cause—he didn't have to participate.

"Give me that." Roman swiped the drink out of his brother's hand and downed what was left. The burn was exactly what he'd sought, but it wasn't nearly enough to curb his nervousness. "Is there more of this somewhere? I could use another."

Derrick slung his arm over Roman's shoulder. "You're fine. It's practically over. Just one more trip out onto that stage, a few women bid on you, you say hello, make some small talk, then plan for a dinner date. There are worse things."

Roman drew in a deep breath through his nose. Of course he knew that everything his brother was saying was true. It still didn't help. "I don't like being the center of attention. You know that. There is so much press out there. The thought makes me sick."

Derrick sighed and patted Roman's lapel. "I know. And I get it. But there are socialites out there, and a whole bunch of actors and models. The photographers will chase after them. I doubt you'll garner much attention."

Roman's history with the media was a long one, and no part of it was pleasant. He'd found that the only way to stay out of their crosshairs was to remain in the shadows and fiercely protect his privacy. It was only out of love and devotion to his brother and sister-in-law that he'd agreed to the auction. "I really hope you're right."

"I'm going to head out and grab my seat. Good luck." Derrick gave Roman a quick hug.

"I don't even know what good luck would look like, but thanks."

Derrick departed and Roman paced backstage, waiting for his turn. The sounds coming from the auction were nothing more than white noise in the background, drowned out by the thoughts tumbling through his own head. He had work he could be doing right now. His newest hotel project, a property he and Derrick were developing together here in Manhattan, was taking a great deal of his time, but it was also immensely rewarding. Derrick and Roman were best friends and incredibly close. Derrick had gotten Roman through his most difficult period, when Roman was in his early twenties and his entire life fell apart. He'd lost the only woman he'd ever loved in a tragic accident, only to discover after her death that she'd betrayed him. To make it worse, an unscrupulous journalist discovered the salacious details and did his best to make Roman's life a living hell. Every step of the way, Derrick was there to help Roman fend off the press while he came to terms with the loss and the lies. Eventually, he also helped him hide those falsehoods and bury them forever.

A stagehand with a clipboard and a headset approached Roman. "Mr. Scott," she said. "You're up next."

"Great." *Let's get this over with.* "Anything I need to know?"

"Smile and look pretty?"

Roman laughed quietly. "I'll do my best." He stood at the opening of the curtain and when his name was announced, the stagehand pulled the fabric back for him. Taking long strides, he arrived at center stage. The presence of his sister-in-law, Fiona, helped to calm his nerves.

"Now, ladies, we have a very special guy up for bid next. My very handsome, enormously successful and perpetually single brother-in-law, Roman Scott."

Roman smiled and waved, willing time to go faster.

"Just as we have with the other gentlemen, we'll start the bidding at twenty-five thousand."

A blond woman in the front row stuck her paddle up straight in the air. "Twenty-five," she called.

"Twenty-six," a brunette woman several rows behind her said.

The blonde crossed her legs and thrust up her paddle again. The slit of her dress opened, revealing an alluring stretch of shapely skin. "Thirty."

For the first time that night, Roman found himself enjoying the attention. The woman in the front row, with shoulder-length honey hair and wearing a gold dress, was breathtakingly beautiful. And she had an air about her that said she was *not* to be messed with. He liked that. A lot.

"Thirty-five," the second woman countered.

"Fifty," the blonde said immediately.

The crowd grew quiet. "Oh, my, Roman. There seems to be a bidding war," Fiona tittered.

"Fifty-five." A third woman joined the fray from somewhere in the depths of the room.

Followed by a fourth woman. "Sixty."

Roman was reeling. There really was a bidding war. Fiona had told him that this sometimes happened, when bidders became so wrapped up in beating each other that it drove up the price. He hadn't given the idea a second thought at the time. He'd been certain he would not become the subject of such a scenario.

The second woman returned to the action with a bid of seventy-five. Another hush fell over the room.

"The bid is seventy-five thousand dollars, which will tie for the highest winning bid in our auction's history. Do I have any other bidders?" Fiona asked, surveying the crowd. "Okay, then. Seventy-five thousand. Going once…going twice…"

"Two hundred," the blonde called.

The entire audience gasped.

"Oh. Wow," Fiona said.

Roman's heart jumped up into his throat. Apparently the beguiling woman in the gold dress was serious about wanting to win a date with him. Far, far worse things had happened. But he also sensed a commotion with the photographers off to the side of the stage. And with a winning bid more than double the record, he might be in for a bad ending to his night.

"That is absolutely wonderful," Fiona said. "Do I have any other competing bids?" She looked out into the room, then turned back to his high-bidding blonde. "Going once...going twice. Sold for two hundred thousand dollars." Fiona kissed Roman on the cheek and peered up at him. "You're doing this auction every year from now on, okay?"

Roman shook his head. "Next year I'll write you a check instead."

Fiona smiled. "Seriously. Thank you. Now go meet your lovely winner."

Roman was dazed as he descended the stairs on the side of the stage and walked up to the woman. With every step closer, her beauty came into sharper view and his brain became a little hazier. Why would such a stunning woman spend so much money to go out with him? Unfortunately, he didn't have time to ponder the answers. Photographers swarmed them, snapping pictures in a frenzy. "Come on," he blurted. With a well-honed reflex, he took her hand and started off for the back of the ballroom.

"Where are we going?" She was doing an impressive job keeping up with him, but she also sounded annoyed.

Roman had no time for conversation. He needed to get away from the press. Everything in his body was telling him to run. He wound himself and the woman through the crowd, moving empty chairs to create obstacles, and zigzagging to make it more difficult for anyone to follow them. "We need to get away from the vultures. Is that okay?"

"If you just stand for a few pictures, they'll go away." She came to a halt, which nearly pulled his arm out of the socket.

He saw them closing in. An old familiar panic rose in his throat like acid. "No. We have to go now." He didn't wait for her to argue this time, rushing out the side door, and leaving her to chase after him.

"Will you please slow down?" she yelled, managing to keep close as he thundered down the escalator, past bewildered riders.

"There's no time. We have to get away from them." He grasped her hand again and they jogged through the lobby, out the hotel entrance, then down the sidewalk.

"It's just the tabloids. I'm used to them by now. They're always hounding my friends and me," she said breathlessly.

He hurried around the corner, wondering who this woman was. He'd ask as soon as he had the chance.

"Don't make excuses for them." Ahead, Roman spotted his driver, standing near his limo. He glanced back over his shoulder and could see that they were still being followed. "Do you have anywhere you need to be right now? Because my driver is at the end of the block and I think it's best if we simply get out of here."

"Why do I feel like I don't have a choice? I'm afraid that if I let you go, I'll never see you again."

Now Roman felt bad. He'd have to explain his reaction. At some point. "I promise to make it worth your while." He grabbed her hand and sprinted for the limo. His driver had the door open already, and feeling a great sense of urgency, Roman helped her inside by planting his hand firmly on her butt and pushing.

She landed with a plop on the seat, her dress billowing up around her. Roman climbed in next to her and closed the door as his driver hustled around to the front of the car.

"Is that what you meant by making it worth my while?" She blew her hair out of her face, trying to tamp down the voluminous skirt of her dress.

Heat flooded his cheeks as the limo sped away. "No. I'm sorry. That was an accident." Despite his embarrassment, he was relieved they'd avoided a run-in with the press.

She shook her head. "I can't believe I paid nearly a quarter of a million dollars so I could run down a sidewalk in heels and have you grab my ass."

"Why, exactly, *did* you make such a ridiculous

bid? That's the entire reason those photographers decided to follow us."

"Some men would be flattered." She delivered a look that suggested he was ridiculous.

He sucked in a deep breath as his heart rate returned to normal and the power of the adrenaline coursing through his veins began to fade. "I'm sorry. I am flattered. Truly. I am. But I'm also perplexed. I don't know who you are, but I can't imagine you have any problem meeting men or finding dates."

"Excuse me? You don't know me at all."

"Look at you." His gaze connected with hers and it felt a bit like she could see right through him. "You're beautiful."

Her lips pressed together tightly, but she didn't appear to be fighting a smile. It was more like she was trying not to grimace. "Thank you, but I don't need you to say things like that to me, okay?"

"Okay…"

"And for the record, being beautiful or pretty or even merely cute doesn't mean you have a decent love life."

Roman sensed there was more to that, but they'd only just met and he wasn't about to pry. "Point taken."

"Look. I paid quite a lot for a sliver of time with you and I intend to get my money's worth."

"What does that mean, exactly?"

She turned to him and extended her hand. "My name is Taylor Klein and I have spent the last several weeks trying to get to you."

"Get to me? I don't understand."

"I need you for your brain. And your creativity."

"So you don't want to go out to dinner with me?"

She sat back in her seat. "Not particularly. Especially not if you're thinking about wine and candles and all of that."

Roman couldn't have been more confused—or intrigued—if he tried. This exquisite woman didn't want romance? She only wanted his mind? "Okay, then. Tell me more."

Two

"Home, Mr. Scott?" Roman's driver asked.

"Yes," he answered, seeming distracted as he loosened his bow tie. He then undid the top three buttons of his crisp white dress shirt, revealing a peek of enticing chest—smooth skin with a light tawny hue.

Taylor made a point of looking out the window. Men were her absolute downfall. More than a weakness, they were the source of nearly every misery she'd ever had in her life. Roman held a lot of power over her. He was a dead-sexy man whose help she needed to start her new business venture. *Eyes on the prize, not on the guy.*

"I hope that's okay with you," he said to Taylor. "We can go up to my place and have a drink and chat about why exactly you need me for my brain and creativity."

If Taylor had a dollar for every time she'd been invited upstairs to a man's apartment, she'd nearly pay off the bid she'd made for Roman in the bachelor auction. She'd fallen prey to promises of small-batch bourbon, smooth talk about art or the theater, and handsome faces dotted with stubble who thought little of seducing a woman and later casting her aside. It never ended well, but the last breakup had been the worst. Ian. And it all started with an invitation to his place. *Just for a drink.* Still, Taylor was not going to be put off track by her past. She would accept this invitation, knowing exactly what she needed to avoid—giving in to a kiss, taking off her dress and falling into bed. "That's fine. As long as you understand that this is business. Nothing else."

"I've never done a bachelor auction before, but I was under the impression that women made bids so that they could actually go on a date with a man."

Taylor had done extensive research on Roman, but the only details she'd been able to unearth were those relating to his hotels and other properties. Aside from learning that he had a brother, she'd obtained almost no personal facts about him. It was as if the man didn't have a personal life. Like he was a ghost. "I've never attended a bachelor auction, either, if you must know. So I guess I'm unaware of the protocol."

"They're a little absurd, don't you think?"

"I don't plan to go to another one anytime soon

if that's what you're asking. The whole thing felt strange. I'm sure it felt awkward to be on that stage."

"It did. Incredibly so. I don't like being in the spotlight. I'd rather stay in the background and get my work done."

She glanced over at him as he scrubbed his face with his long fingers. Roman was a mystery wrapped up in a delicious package. He had the most impressive bone structure she'd ever seen—an angular jaw and strong chin. His eyes were intense, but they were also guarded. He wouldn't hold her gaze for more than a second or two before he looked away. If the hotel business hadn't panned out so well for him, she could imagine that he would've made a highly successful model if he'd been so inclined. He had the trim build and straight shoulders for it, and the height as well. But it was clear that his demeanor never would've allowed him to pursue a career based on being the center of attention.

"Interesting," Taylor said, tucking her hair behind her ears and settling back in the seat.

"Interesting how?"

Part of her was hesitant to be plain about what she was thinking. She wanted Roman on her good side. But she did find his personality to be incongruous with what she knew of wealthy, powerful men. The whole thing was curious. She turned to him, angling her body in his direction. It meant that her knees were only a few inches from his long legs, and even with her in a full-length gown and him in his black tuxedo trousers, she found the proximity to be a little too exciting. "I think it's interesting that a self-made man who is the sole owner of seventeen world-renowned hotels doesn't want to stand in the spotlight. Most successful people, especially men, soak up that stuff like they need it to live."

"Not me." He cleared his throat and went very still as he watched her with a critical squint. "Is that what you want from me? A job? Something having to do with my hotels?"

"I don't want a job. I'm done with having a boss. I want to be in charge of my own destiny." She hoped she didn't sound wide-eyed or naive, but she'd had it with working for anyone else. She wasn't about to disclose how her last job had ended, but needless to say, it hadn't been her finest moment. "That's why I want to turn my family's summer estate in Connecticut into a boutique hotel. But I don't believe in doing things halfway, and that's where you come in. I need your advice about what to do with the property, and ideas about development of the grounds. I'd also love to get some pointers on marketing and positioning."

"It's now my turn to say *interesting*."

"Why?"

"No one's ever asked me for that kind of advice before. Ever."

"How is that possible?"

"I don't know."

"Maybe people are too intimidated by you. Or they don't appreciate your brilliance."

He cast another sideways glance at her. It sent a

thrill right through her, like a warm and powerful gust of air when a summer storm is about to roll in. "You don't have to butter me up. You've paid more than enough for this conversation."

"It's not flattery. It's the truth."

Before Taylor could elaborate, she noticed that Roman's driver was slowing the car down to a crawl as they passed one of the most exclusive apartment buildings in all of Manhattan, right on Park Avenue in the center of what was known as Billionaires' Row.

"Dammit," Roman muttered, looking out the window. "They're here."

"Who's here?" Taylor said.

"The press. I'm afraid your outlandish bid put me in their crosshairs."

Taylor wasn't the type of person to shrink or fawn, and even though the stern tone of Roman's voice was a bit too close to her dad's, she wasn't about to put up with words like *outlandish*. "If you returned phone calls, you might not be in this predicament. If you hadn't ignored the dozens of messages I left for you, I might not be out a sizable chunk of the money I want to use for my hotel."

Roman's driver lowered the partition between himself and the back of the limo. "Sir? I've checked with security and the parking garage is secure. I suggest we go inside now while the coast is clear."

"Yes. Go." Roman sat back in his seat, seeming fitful and annoyed. "Exactly why would I call back a woman I don't know? I'm a very busy man. I have a massive business to oversee."

"I thought the Klein name would be enough to make you return my call. My father's investment firm has held multiple corporate retreats at your properties. They've spent hundreds of thousands of dollars with you. At least. Maybe more."

He turned and placed a hand on her arm. "Hold on a minute. You're Walter Klein's daughter?"

Taylor bristled at his words. They were a stark reminder of what she'd failed to achieve. She didn't want to be merely known as someone's daughter. She wanted to make her mark on the world and be known for her own achievements. But those were thoughts that were hard to formulate into words when she was enjoying this bit of physical contact much more than she wanted to. "Yes. He's my dad."

"Why didn't you say that when you left a message?"

"Honestly, I was hoping you'd be smart enough to figure it out. I guess you just weren't curious about it."

He cast her another disgruntled glance. "I'm plenty curious. Everything I've built is because I always want to know more. To learn. It's my assistant who isn't. She fields calls and requests from hundreds of people a day. If she doesn't know you and you don't give her a point of reference, she'll move on."

"So you're saying the message never even reached you?"

"No. It did not."

Frustration at the assumptions she'd made threatened to eat Taylor alive. But she'd made plenty of mistakes before in her life. This was simply another one on the list. "Well, I don't feel very smart right now."

"Mr. Scott?" his driver asked.

Roman peered out through the window. "Looks okay to me."

"Me too, sir," his driver responded. "I'll get your door." A few seconds later, Roman's side of the car was open and only ten or fifteen feet ahead was an elevator.

Roman climbed out then reached for Taylor's hand. "Come on."

She stumbled out of the car. If this was what it was like to travel with Roman Scott, Taylor might take a pass next time. She'd been jostled more times than she cared to think about. The driver marched ahead the several paces to the elevator. He swiped a pass in front of an electronic pad, the doors immediately whooshed open and he held them for Roman and Taylor while he scanned the parking garage for… something. Presumably, the press.

Roman shook his head and pinched the bridge of his nose as the elevator began to climb.

"Do you mind if I ask why all the cloak and dagger?" She truly didn't understand. To her, photographers and the media were annoying, but mostly harmless. Everyone had a right to earn a living. "Are you in some kind of trouble I don't know about? Is there some scandal brewing?"

"I've devoted years to keeping my personal life

out of the newspapers. I'm not about to let it happen now." His stern tone returned. Apparently, Taylor was going to have to get used to that. She was also pretty determined to never ask that question again. It was too much like poking a grumpy bear. But it did explain why there was absolutely no dirt to be found about him.

The elevator came to a stop and the doors opened. "Is this our stop?"

"It is."

Taylor stepped inside. She'd been in dozens of penthouse apartments in her life, several of them owned by friends and family members, a few occupied by boyfriends who hadn't lasted very long. But this one was absolutely jaw-dropping. They'd entered a round foyer with a white marble floor and several entryways. One to the left, one to the right, and the widest was straight ahead, revealing what appeared to be a living room far beyond it, with a near-panoramic view of the city at night. Lights of all colors twinkled against a blue-black background. It was magical and breathtaking. And so sexy. "What floor are we on?"

"Eighty-four." Roman rolled his arms out of his tux jacket and yanked his tie from the collar of his shirt, then tossed it aside on a table.

"Whoa." Taylor reflexively reached for the nearest wall.

Roman turned to her, his eyes even darker in the softly lit space. "Are you okay?"

She pulled back her hand, feeling silly. "Sorry.

I'm really scared of heights. I guess it didn't seem like we were on the elevator for very long. And my ears usually pop when I go up this high."

"It's high-speed, and the cabin is pressurized for comfort."

"Oh. Nice."

"A drink, then?" He waved his hand in invitation for her to walk through the central doorway.

"Uh. Sure." She nodded, but was definitely not thrilled with the idea of getting any closer to the city view ahead, no matter how beautiful it might be.

Her hesitancy seemed to amuse Roman. "It's okay. Nothing will happen to you in the living room. You aren't going to fall out of the building. I swear."

She took a deep breath and forced a smile. She knew her fear was nonsensical, but that was the thing about fears—they often defied explanation. "I just need a second." The embarrassment she felt was growing by the minute. She was once again blowing it. *Get it together, Taylor.*

Roman reached for her. "Come on. I promise I will walk you into that room and sit you down as far from the windows as possible. A few sips of a cocktail and you should feel much better."

She looked at his hand, afraid to trust him or his words. But this was part of moving forward in her life, so she extended her arm and allowed him to wrap up her fingers in his.

"Better?"

She nodded and took a step. His hand was indeed a comfort, warm and solid. "Yes. Thank you."

He was as patient as could be, easing them into the room at a speed she'd figured she was saving for maybe her seventies or eighties. As soon as they reached the room, Roman flipped on a few low lights over a bar area to the right, then sat her down in a generous white-upholstered chair. "What can I get for you?"

"What do you have?"

"Anything and everything." He smiled for the first time since he'd been on that stage, but this expression was different. It was natural and warm. Not forced.

"Gin and tonic?"

"What kind of gin? And lemon or lime?"

"Hendrick's. And lime, of course. What person puts lemon in their gin and tonic?" she asked, feeling a bit more comfortable as she settled back in the chair and was able to finally take a deep breath—and take stock of where she was—in Roman Scott's apartment, ready to ask him hundreds of questions, exactly where she'd hoped to be.

"You'd be surprised at some people's drink order."

Taylor had to wonder if the people he was speaking of were women. Although she'd had so little luck finding out about his personal life, surely a man so handsome and wealthy had women in endless pursuit of him. As he turned his back to her and went to tending bar, she stole this chance to admire a side of him she had not yet studied—the rear view. A silent hum of approval bubbled up from her throat as her eyes raked across his shoulders and down his long torso to what was an objectively incredible ass.

Too bad he was not hers to touch. If she was smart, no guy was, but especially not Roman. He was far too tempting on every level.

"Here we are." He turned and approached her with two drinks in hand. Their fingers brushed as he delivered the ice-cold glass and raised his to toast. "To bachelor auctions?"

Taylor laughed quietly. At least the mood had lightened somewhat. "Yes. It worked out for me. And your sister-in-law's foundation."

Roman sat in the chair opposite her and took a sip of what looked to be bourbon or scotch, allowing the single ice cube to rattle in the glass. "So, Ms. Klein. What exactly do you want to know? How did you envision this working?"

She sat a little straighter and scooted forward to the edge of her seat. "I was hoping you'd meet with me a few times. As I work through the project. I figure a dinner and drinks has to count for three hours. So I'd like to have that much of your time if I can get it." She cleared her throat, preparing herself to voice the bigger ask. "And actually, I was hoping I could convince you to come up to Connecticut."

Roman hadn't heard such a bold suggestion in some time. And if Taylor wasn't so breathtaking, and interesting, he might have laughed it away. "I'm listening."

"My family has owned the estate for years. Since the early 1900s. The house that's standing on the property now was built in 1919, but there was an original house built in 1902 that burned down."

"Thanks for the history lesson, but I'm still not sure why this means I need to go to Connecticut." He didn't want to go on and on about how busy he was, but his schedule was packed. In fact, sitting here in his own living room with Taylor, he realized that he hadn't had a relaxed conversation with anyone in quite some time. Sure, this revolved around work, but there was very little pressure on him. He didn't have any skin in the game, and could afford to sit back and be academic about his high-pressure business. Of course, being around Taylor was its own challenge. Her beauty was that breathtaking. Her presence was that intriguing. The irony of it all was that he sensed that she didn't see any of this in herself. Which seemed like a real shame.

"The property is beautiful and sprawling, but the house is a bit outdated. I was hoping that I could work with the shell of the building, but add a modern and eclectic feel to the interiors. And then move on to building individual bungalows or cottages as the hotel takes off. Eventually build a real escape."

"And you plan to run this on your own?" He took a sip of his drink, relishing the burn of the bourbon as it drifted down his throat. "All by yourself up in Connecticut? No more New York for you? Assuming you live here in Manhattan. You've told me very little about yourself, Taylor Klein."

"I do live in New York, but I'm ready for a change. There are too many ghosts in this city for me. I could use some different scenery. And the property really is lovely. Very serene and peaceful. I don't know about you, but the city gets to me sometimes."

"I can appreciate the thought. For sure." If only she knew how much it got to him. It was part of why he lived so high above it. Being closer to the clouds was the only way to get any tranquility here. "Your parents are okay with you turning one of the family retreats into a business?"

She nodded eagerly. "They are. We have plenty of vacation homes. And my dad is leading the charge. He just wants me to be happy. And to be successful."

Roman's knowledge of Taylor's father wasn't quite so warm and fuzzy, but he imagined that the man could be much kinder to his own daughter.

"Does that mean you'll come up and see it? I know you're a very busy man, and I'm sure your schedule is impossible, but it would mean so much to me. I've loved your hotels from the very first time I stayed in one. And at the end of that trip, I made a point of visiting every single one."

Roman was not used to the idea of having a fan. He wasn't a rock star or a famous actor or anyone who generally attracted this kind of attention. But everything Taylor was saying made it sound as though she truly appreciated the work he did. He'd rarely had that kind of positive reinforcement. Appreciation. Usually, it was his bank account that told him he was doing okay. It was nice to hear kind and generous words from such a vibrant and energetic woman. "Careful. You'll make me blush."

"People only blush when they know that the compliment is true." She finished her statement with a flirtatious bounce of her eyebrows.

Everything below Roman's waist went tight. Heat crept up his stomach. He slugged down the last of his drink, pondering her proposition…and her. She was fun and smart and, he could imagine, quite impossible to resist. That last part concerned him, but not too greatly. It had been a while since a woman had captured his imagination in this way. It made him feel alive to experience it again. Too much of his life was living in the never-ending loop of nurturing his empire while trying to build more. How much would ever be enough? He could retire tomorrow and be happy. But he'd sadly be alone. "How long do you need?"

"I could be satisfied with twenty-four hours."

Satisfied. That was an interesting choice of words. He watched as the tip of her tongue rolled onto her lower lip. He could be deeply satisfied by a kiss from Taylor. A long, hot passionate kiss. The kind that you wanted to go on for days. "What if I try for more than satisfied? What would it take to make you happy?"

Her smile lit up the entire room, which was saying a lot in the opulent and expansive space. "Three days?"

He swallowed hard. His assistant was going to kill him when he announced that his entire schedule would need to be reworked. Then again, he hadn't taken off any time in years. And it was a Friday. Which really only meant that his Monday would need to be shuffled to other days. It was a small price to pay to help someone as enthusiastic as Taylor. "We don't need to let anyone know ahead of time that we're coming?"

"Nope. We have a caretaker who has it ready at all times. He's new to the job, but my entire family loves him."

"Oh, great."

"So you'll do it?"

He finished off his drink and placed his glass on the low cocktail table between them. "I will. As long as we can leave tonight."

Taylor's eyes went wide with shock. "Now?"

Roman got up from his seat and took his glass over to the bar to give it a quick rinse. "Yes, Taylor. My schedule is packed. It's now or never."

Just then, Taylor's phone beeped with a text. Then beeped again.

"Go ahead and check it. But you only have a few minutes to give me an answer. Otherwise, I'm going to bed."

Taylor scrambled to dig her phone out of her evening bag. "Oh, no." She looked up at him, her face painted with abject horror.

"What is it? Did someone die?" His mind went to all sorts of terrible places, but that was merely his history rearing its ugly head.

She shook her head. "I'm afraid to tell you."

"Well, now you *have* to tell me." He walked over until he was standing at her side. He peered down at her, trying to keep himself from being utterly mesmerized by her chest, her shimmery skin and the way that glittery gold dress put her cleavage on stunning display.

"It's the tabloids. They wrote about us. There's a picture of us running down the sidewalk away from the auction."

He held out his hand and she surrendered her phone. He didn't bother to read the full article. He merely glanced at the photo, the headline, and knew he'd seen enough. *Socialite Pays Big Bucks for Billionaire.* His mind immediately went to what came next. The press would hound him. If history served as any yardstick, it would likely be for the next forty-eight hours. Unless something else big and ugly reared its head, like if someone decided to do a deep dive into his past. Then that might make it worse. Photographers would stake out his building. They'd be in front of his office on Monday morning. They would sneak into the parking garage and hide next to his car. They'd try to bribe his housekeeper. They would be everywhere. His only comfort right now was that he could outrun them. He could escape. He had the means, and thanks to Taylor, he had a place to go to that no one would ever expect.

He returned her phone. "Doesn't really surprise me."

"I'm so sorry. I don't even know what to say." She got up from her chair, and standing that close to each other, especially after the soft buzz of the bourbon had made its way through his body, all he wanted to do was take her in his arms and kiss her. He could hide away in this apartment. That was the safe and easy choice. But that wasn't going to give Taylor what she wanted. And something deep inside him was saying that wasn't what he wanted, either.

"Don't apologize. It's not your fault. They take one little bit of tawdriness and turn it into more. That's what they do."

"I'd hardly call a bachelor auction tawdry."

"For the amount of money you paid?" he asked. "I'm sure everyone and their mother is assuming that you and I are naked, right now, in my bed. I suppose I should thank you for that. I don't know that I've been seen in such a flattering light in quite some time."

The look of horror on her face morphed to embarrassment. Her cheeks bloomed with pink. She pressed her hand to her luscious lips. "Do you really think that's what people think?"

It was certainly what he was thinking. Or hoping. "Probably. People want to believe only the most salacious things."

"So what do we do now? Do you still want to go to Connecticut?"

"I think that's actually our best move right now. Yes."

"Will your driver take us? Can he swing by my place so I can pack a bag?"

Roman plucked Taylor's drink from the table and handed it to her. "Here. Finish up."

She slugged down the last of it and returned the glass. "So?"

"No, my driver won't be taking us. And no, we can't swing by your place so you can pick up a bag."

He pulled his phone out of his pocket and typed out a quick text. An affirmative reply came immediately, which he expected, because that was what he paid for—exceptional service.

"I don't understand."

"We'll be traveling by air. Helicopter to be exact. They'll be up on the building's helipad in fifteen minutes."

"Oh. No. No. I don't think I can do that." Her voice was high and panicked.

Roman hadn't considered her fear of heights. "Don't worry. My pilot has a great deal of experience. You'll be completely safe."

"What about my stuff? I can't wear this for three days." With both hands, she lifted the skirt of her dress a few inches then dropped it.

"I don't see why not. I'd love to see you in that dress for three days." *And I wouldn't mind seeing you out of it.*

"This is a little more spur of the moment than I planned on." She looked around the room, seeming frantic. "I mean, I do have some clothes up there. But not a lot. Some of it I haven't worn in years."

"It'll be like a stroll down memory lane."

"This is not how I pictured tonight playing out." She delivered a piercing gaze, her eyes blazing with intensity. It was so hot it nearly burned him to the ground.

"Me neither, Taylor. Me neither."

Three

This is unbelievable. Absolutely absurd. Those thoughts were about as complex as Taylor could manage right now.

"Is your seat belt comfortable? Too tight?" Roman asked.

Despite the rotor blades spinning impossibly fast overhead, she could hear her own heartbeat, pounding fiercely in her ears. She was petrified. She'd honestly never been more scared in all her life. She nodded at Roman's question, even when she should have been shaking her head. "Yeah. I think it's okay."

He leaned in closer, and that was when she got an amazing whiff of his cologne. It was warm like bourbon, but with woodsy notes like cedar. "You will be okay. I promise. I swear on everything I hold dear."

"Okay."

The rotors sped up and the helicopter lurched, rising a few feet, dropping down a bit, then pitching forward and veering off into the sky over Manhattan. Taylor clamped her eyes shut and wrapped her arms around her waist as her stomach got light and fluttery then sank down into her body. *You're okay. You're okay.* She tried not to think about where she was. About what she was doing, essentially hanging over the city in a flying tin can. Panic threatened to climb up into her throat. Her heart was beating too fast. A headache started to brew. And then she felt warmth.

A hand. On hers.

She turned and dared to open one eye to peek at Roman. She kept her sights trained on his handsome face, too frightened to look at the inky night sky outside the windows.

"I don't want you to be scared. Not with me."

Good God, he was irresistible, and she had such a weakness for a man who wasn't afraid to be protective. What in the world was she doing, heading off to her family's estate for three days? Where they were going to be all alone. *All. Alone.* She wasn't thinking straight. Her track record with men suggested that it would take twenty minutes after landing before she was kissing him and taking off her clothes. Thirty minutes, tops. *This is for your future.* She became keenly aware of their hands, intertwined. But tried to think of the intimate gesture as chaste, even when it didn't feel that way. "Thank you. I'm sorry I'm so nervous. I've been like this since I was a kid."

"But you've ridden in a helicopter before."

"I have. A few times. Not many. My family all know how much I hate it, so it's only in extreme circumstances that we travel this way."

"How many in your family?"

"It's just my mom and dad and my older brother, Jeremy."

"Are your parents still together? I feel like that doesn't happen much in certain circles."

Taylor knew what he was doing and she appreciated it greatly. He was trying to distract her. So she continued the conversation. "You're so right. When there's a lot of money involved, it seems like men trade their wives for newer models, which only leads their wives to do the same." It might have sounded like a cliché, but it was absolutely true. "Luckily, my parents are very happy together. Still very much in love after more than thirty-five years."

"Wow. That's a long time."

"It is. My brother is thirty-three. And I'm thirty-one. That makes it pretty easy to keep track of."

Roman swallowed so hard she saw his Adam's apple bob up and down. "I'm nearly ten years older than you."

Was that a warning? It sounded a bit like it might be, as Roman wanted her to understand that they were not a good idea, even when everything he did only seemed to be about pulling her closer. "Ten years is nothing." As to why she was making a case for their age difference not mattering, she wasn't sure. She only knew that to her, it wasn't a problem. Men, romance and sex were the real trouble for Taylor. Age? No big deal.

It wasn't long before she felt the helicopter descending. The pilot buzzed the cabin. "Sir? Is there a landing pad?"

Roman looked to Taylor for an answer.

"The yard behind the house. It's got to be a good acre or two with no trees. Completely flat. That's the spot my dad uses if he ever arrives that way from the city."

"Did you get that?" Roman asked the pilot.

"Copy," he answered. "We'll be on the ground in a few minutes."

"See? I told you everything would be fine."

Now she was starting to feel nervous in a different way, more of a surge of excitement than anything else. They were about to shift into the scenario where she was the host, and it was on her to make sure he was comfortable and happy. It also meant it was time for her to start soaking up his brilliance, commit every word to memory and learn from it all. Then she could find the success she'd long wanted. Then she could finally be on the right track.

A large bright light shined from under the helicopter, illuminating the grassy expanse of the backyard of the family estate. The drop to the ground was slow and smooth, and with every inch closer to earth, Taylor felt herself relax a little more. When they finally landed, she blew out a long and heavy breath. *Safe and sound. Just like he'd promised.*

A few moments later, the rotors slowed and the pilot was there to open the door for them. Roman grabbed his bag from the seat opposite them and was the first to hop out. He reached for Taylor's hand as she did her best climbing out of a helicopter in a fluffy full-length gown and heels.

Roman spoke to the pilot for a moment. Something about Monday. And that meant Taylor knew her timeline. She had Saturday and Sunday to get what she needed out of Roman Scott. It was best that she got right down to business.

They marched up the gentle slope of the lawn to the house, where the curved bank of French doors gracefully hugged the pool and flagstone patio. Taylor went to the far left door, where there was an electronic keypad. She entered the code, then stepped inside and disarmed the house alarm in the mudroom, then led Roman into the kitchen.

"Looks like someone was prepared for our arrival." Roman nodded to a bottle of red wine in the center of the large marble-topped island, which was accompanied by a note.

Let me know if you need anything.—Bruce

"It's our caretaker. I texted him from your apartment to let him know I was coming up to the house a few days early." She walked over to the Sub-Zero fridge and opened the door. Inside was a full compliment of groceries. On the counter was a loaf of bread from the bakery in town. Bruce was wonderful at his job. He always took care of every little thing. "Can I get you something to drink?"

"I wouldn't say no to a glass of that wine."

"Sounds perfect." Taylor went to the cabinet and pulled out two wineglasses, then grabbed the corkscrew from a drawer. She carefully poured two glasses and handed one to him. "To me never going on another helicopter."

Roman smirked and clinked his glass with hers. "Don't count on it. The one thing I've learned is that you never know what the future holds."

"True. But I'm pretty sure I know what I will do anything to avoid." She kicked off her shoes. "Come on. Let's go sit in the study. It's much more comfortable."

"Lead the way."

Taylor did exactly that, down the grand central hall, with its twelve-foot coffered ceilings dripping with a procession of crystal chandeliers, and to the side, along the walls, black velvet–tufted settees, which Taylor had always assumed were for fainting. Beneath their feet were original mahogany wood floors with fleurs-de-lis inlaid at every corner. There was a lot she loved about this house. It was steeped in family history. And she appreciated the high quality of the materials and the craftsmanship it had taken to create it all. But she was definitely ready to update it and make it much more hip. She was eager to transform it into her own creation.

"We're in here." Taylor stepped into one of several studies in the house. "I think this was originally the cigar room. But my grandmother despised cigars and never let anyone smoke in the house."

Roman surveyed the room, taking it all in. "I see potential here. Certainly. Although you will have to make changes. A lot of them."

Taylor walked over to flip on the gas fireplace at the far corner of the room. The flames leaped to life, flickering and casting the room in a warm glow. She gestured to one of two leather club chairs. "Please have a seat."

"Gas is a pretty modern convenience for a house this old."

"My dad had these put in a few years ago. He hated having to get up every twenty minutes to poke at the fire. And he hated even more the idea of paying someone else to do it."

Roman took a seat, crossing his long legs and staring into the fire. Taylor perched herself in the chair next to him, realizing just how tired she was, and feeling utterly ridiculous in her dress. She hoped she had something suitable to sleep in upstairs, but she'd worry about that when she went to bed. For now, a glass of wine and some quiet conversation were in order.

"You said you told the caretaker you were coming early," Roman said. "You were already planning to come up here?"

She nodded. "Yes. That was the plan. Bid on you at the auction, win you, then arrange a meeting so we could talk business, hopefully right away, so that I could come up here next week and get to work."

He laughed quietly. "You realize your plan was extremely optimistic. A lot could have gone wrong."

"I knew I had a lot I could put on the line."

"You mean money."

It occurred to her then that she was risking more than a chunk of her budget on Roman. She was putting herself and her heart in peril. Her attraction to him was undeniable, and she suspected that with every minute together over the next couple of days, he would only become more irresistible. She could imagine that every brilliant piece of advice would make her want him more. She would have to do her best to stay on high alert. Fight hard to maintain distance. Remain professional. "Yes. Money."

"You could've gotten me for cheaper. Those other women were going to stand down at some point."

Taylor's cheeks flushed with embarrassment. "I guess I went overboard."

"You guess?"

"I can't help it. I'm supercompetitive. And there was something about those other women vying for what I wanted that made me nuts. With every counterbid, I became that much more determined to bury them."

"And so you did. In a pile of money."

"With a bid that ended up sending our night into a tailspin."

One corner of his mouth quirked up in a near grin. "Despite all that, I'm enjoying myself. You and your

ambition intrigue me, Taylor. I look forward to working on your project over the weekend."

She was relieved that he'd brought up her ambition. Any mention of business was a good thing. A
tiny guardrail to help keep her on the right track.
"Oh, good. I'm glad."

"Then I have to go back on Monday."

"Big project?"

"Something with my brother. I'm not really at lib-
erty to discuss it."

"Oh, sure. Of course." Yes, she'd made inroads
with Roman, but there were some things that she
wasn't going to be made privy to. There were likely
quite a lot of trade secrets locked up in his handsome
head, and she'd be lucky to convince him to share
even a fraction of them. If she played her cards right,
respected his boundaries, and this weekend went
well, he could end up being a source of business advice for quite a long time. She hoped for that. Greatly.

The grandfather clock in the corner of the room
chimed. "Oh, wow. It's one a.m."

"Probably time to head to bed."

Taylor hated the way her mind instantly went to
the idea of Roman in her bed. *Cut it out.* "Yes. I'll
show you upstairs to your room."

Roman gathered his bag and Taylor led him up
the grand Elizabethan spiral staircase. The bay of
windows surrounding them had always made Taylor
scared when she was a kid. There were no window
treatments, and at this time of night, you could see
nothing but absolute blackness outside. Luckily, by

day, they provided a spectacular view of the estate's circular entrance, with a fountain at center and manicured hedges running along the stone drive leading out to the road. It really was a magical place. And she hoped guests would love coming here. That she would learn to love living here full-time.

At the top of the stairs were three halls—one straight ahead that led to a large home office, and what had once been a playroom; one to the left, which led to the family's bedrooms; and one to the right, where the guest quarters were. Of course, this would all change when she opened the hotel. She flipped on the switch, lighting up the corridor, and walked Roman to the first guest bedroom, where she turned on yet more lights. "I hope this is okay."

He stepped inside and gently placed his bag on the bench at the foot of the bed. He took a quick survey of the decor, which was lovely, but a good decade out of date. "It's nice."

"It needs work."

He slid her a bemused smile. "Okay, fine. It needs work. I didn't want to be rude."

"I appreciate that. I do. But this weekend, I need you to be brutally honest with me." She leaned against the door frame and watched as he sat on the edge of the bed. Again, she found herself warring with her own desire. Why did men like Roman Scott make her feel so weak? "Tell me everything that needs to be fixed. Everything that's wrong. I want to hear it all."

He swished his hand across the fluffy white duvet.

"Bedding is nice. I'm going to hop in the shower in a minute, so I'll tell you tomorrow what I think of the bathroom."

She had to get out of there. Sprint. Run down the hall and lock herself away in her own bedroom. The mental image of Roman's long and lean frame in the shower, with the water beading on his magnificent shoulders, and dripping down from his thick hair. That was going to stick with her all night. She'd probably need a sleeping pill to shake the idea and get some rest. "Sounds great. I'll see you in the morning."

"Good night," he said, getting up from the bed and approaching the doorway. For a moment, she wondered if he was thinking about kissing her. But then he reached for the door.

"Sleep well," she said as Roman closed the door, leaving Taylor to her own devices in the hall. Whatever she did, she had to stop thinking of Roman Scott in any way outside of the professional realm. There would be no kissing this weekend. No flirting. No romance. No showering. *Definitely* no sex.

No matter how badly she wanted it all from him.

Four

Roman woke to the sun through his window, the scent of coffee in the air and a knife in his back. Or at least it felt that way. His muscles were bound so tight they felt like a ball of rubber bands. It had to be the bed. He carefully rolled to his side in the hopes of alleviating the pain, but instead, it sharpened. He groaned. "Dammit." He'd looked forward to a day helping Taylor with her project. This was really going to throw a wrench in things. Just like there was a wrench in his back.

Despite the agony, he forced himself to rally and push up into a seated position. On the nightstand was his phone, the screen coming to life when he nudged it with his hand. He picked it up and used the face

ID to unlock it. The late-night text exchange with his brother was waiting.

Fiona showed me the story about you and Taylor Klein. Is romance in the air?

Derrick and Fiona were always trying to set Roman up with women. It never worked. No. And mind your own business.

Are you with her now?

Do you not know what mind your own business means?

So that's a yes. Two words of advice: be nice.

Bracing himself with a hand on the nightstand, he slowly straightened, then shuffled into the en suite bathroom. He scrounged through his toiletry bag, finding two pain relievers, which he tossed back with a swig of water.

"If I can stretch this out, I'll be fine," he muttered to himself. He'd only had back issues once before, after a game of pickup basketball with several professional players who'd stayed at his hotel in Miami. It had been incredibly fun. And he paid for it the next day by barely being able to walk.

After getting himself to the floor, he rolled out on the luxe carpet in the bedroom, looking up at the ceiling while he pulled his knees to his chest and breathed deeply. His muscles began to gradually unwind.

A knock came at the door. "Roman? Are you up?"

"I am," he croaked. He gradually lowered his legs, rolled to his knees and stood. All things considered, he felt much better. He just needed the painkillers to kick in and he'd be fine.

"Roman?"

"Yes, Taylor. I'm up."

"Oh, good. Good morning," she said through the door. "I heard running water…thought I'd let you know…is ready."

This was ridiculous. He could hardly hear her through the door. So he opened it.

"What was that?" His sights landed on her, and she knocked the breath right out of him. Her blond hair was a sexy, tousled mess tucked behind both ears, drawing attention to her deep brown eyes. She was wearing a short black sundress with skinny straps that showed off her graceful shoulders and the tempting contours of her collarbone.

"Coffee's on."

"Great. I see you found some clothes."

"I see that you lost some."

He froze. He was only wearing pajama pants. Without a shirt, which would have been a good thing to put on before he'd opened the door. "Oh. Yeah. Sorry." Except that he wasn't entirely sorry for his choice of attire, or lack of it. Taylor was stirring up something in him that hadn't come to the surface in so long—deep, undeniable attraction. He endured a repeat of the rush of heat inside of him, starting deep in his belly and spreading to his chest and thighs.

She looked down at her dress. "I hope you know that this is not what I would normally wear to a business meeting."

He opened the door a little wider. "This is exactly what I wear to business meetings."

"So that's how you close those big million-dollar deals." A wry smile crossed her lips and she cocked an eyebrow. "They *are* exceptionally nice pajama pants."

Another ripple of intense heat hit him. "It's important to dress for success."

"It's also important to offer your guest some hospitality. Like I said, coffee is ready and I ran into town and got some fresh croissants from the bakery."

"Ran into town? How long have you been up?"

"Since six."

He was impressed. "Five hours of sleep. That right there is the true hallmark of entrepreneurship."

"Really? Because I've never been able to sleep for very long. Seven hours is pretty much my max."

"Sounds like we're on the same schedule."

"Then let's get going with our day." She lifted her chin as if to challenge him. "I have a million things to show you."

Good God, her enthusiasm and energy was infectious. Plus, he loved how honest and direct she was. Aside from his brother, almost no one was straight up with him. Either they were trying to get something out of him, so they catered to his every whim, or they were afraid of him and therefore shrouded everything in a veil of positivity. "I'll be right down."

"I'll be waiting."

She started down the hall and he took his chance to watch her walk away. Her hair swung from side to side with every step, mirroring the movement of her hips. His hands twitched with the desire to dig his fingers into her curves and pull her against him. In all truth, she couldn't be more effortlessly beautiful, but it wasn't all her gorgeous exterior. The spark inside her was undeniable, and he was drawn to it like a moth to a flame. He'd grown so accustomed to the rhythm of his life—keeping his head down, maintaining a relentless schedule, like a shark that couldn't stop swimming. He knew it was his defense mechanism. His armor. When you were rich, successful and busy, the lackluster parts of your life weren't quite so evident. They stung a little less. It was a perfectly serviceable way to live. But this small taste of what he'd once enjoyed so much—joking and flirting and an easy back-and-forth with a woman was a real eye-opener. Had he been sleepwalking through his life? If so, Taylor was nudging him awake.

He grabbed a T-shirt for Scott Properties, his brother's real estate development company, slipped on a pair of jeans and worked his feet into a pair of running shoes, trying to ignore the way his back fought him as he bent over to tie them. On his way downstairs, he took note of the details of the house— wide custom moldings that would be cost prohibitive to recreate these days, soaring coffered ceilings, and grand corridors that unsubtly hinted that this was a house that had been built with piles and piles of money. It was indeed magnificent, and he did think it was quite promising as Taylor's project, but she was also correct in assessing that it was going to need work. A lot of work. And he wondered if she truly appreciated exactly how draining and exhausting it might end up being.

In the kitchen, Taylor was seated at the island, humming and busily typing on her laptop.

"Something urgent come up since I saw you five minutes ago?" he asked, helping himself to a cup of black coffee in the mug Taylor had set out for him.

"Finally getting around to answering the emails and texts I got after that story about us ran."

"Did a lot of people see it?" His stomach churned at the thought.

"A few friends and acquaintances reached out last night, but a lot more this morning. I think people are just now waking up to it."

"You know, you don't have to say anything at all. It's not really anyone's business."

"Believe me, some people are *not* getting a response. Some people are just being nosy because they don't have anything better to do." She took a sip of her coffee. "No one said anything to you about it?"

"I got a text from my brother late last night. Fiona saw it."

"Makes sense. I heard from my brother. And my dad."

"Oh, no. Your father?" Roman felt horribly embarrassed. *This* was the perfect example of why he hated the tabloids so much. "Is he upset?"

"Quite the opposite. He knew my whole plan so he was excited that you and I were spending time together. He holds you in very high regard."

Roman felt his shoulders relax, although that only drew attention to the way his back was tightening up again. He leaned against the kitchen counter for support. "That's nice to hear."

"Plus, my dad loves all free publicity. He thinks it will help build buzz for the hotel." Her computer chimed and that drew her attention to the screen. He watched as the warm tones drained from her face. She bunched up her lips, then ran her fingers along the trackpad. She clicked and furiously typed something, then closed the lid and sighed.

"Everything okay?"

"An idiot landed in my inbox, but I told him to go away." She forced a smile, a sure sign that she was covering for something.

"Him? Someone bothering you?"

"My ex. He loves it when he hears about some controversy in my life. He pretends to check in, asks how I'm doing, but it's all fake concern. He really just wants to find a reason to stir the pot."

"That's annoying."

"Tell me about it. He was such a jerk when he heard I got fired from my last job."

"Fired?" How was that possible? Taylor seemed nothing less than competent and driven. Plus, she came from a very powerful family. Surely that would give an employer pause.

"I lost my cool with my boss and told him what I actually thought of him."

"Which was?" He didn't like to pry into other people's lives, but he had an intense curiosity about Taylor. He wanted to know everything.

"I told him that he was arrogant and lazy and took credit for the hard work of everyone around him. And also that he had horrendous bad breath and needed to see a doctor."

He had to stifle a smile. Even though he was fairly certain he wouldn't have responded well to such an accusation from an employee of his, how he admired her fire. "I'm starting to see why you want to work for yourself."

"I seriously can't work for anyone else anymore. I have to be my own boss. I'm thinking that's the reason I've had such a hard time finding the right career. I've been going at it all wrong."

"Hopefully we can do something about that this weekend."

"I hope so, too. When do you want to see everything?"

He grabbed a croissant from the bakery box on the island. "I've got breakfast, so I'm ready whenever you are."

She took another sip of her coffee and hopped up from the barstool she'd been sitting on. "Great. Let's do the tour now. I just need to grab some shoes from the mudroom. I'll be right back."

"You know where to find me." He took a bite of the buttery pastry and nearly groaned in ecstasy. It was light and flaky and nothing short of pure heaven. He glanced out through the kitchen window to the lawn where the helicopter had landed last night. Was that really less than twelve hours ago? He felt as though he'd traveled to another dimension, one where his morning consisted of lively breakfast conversation, beautiful company and sublime pastries.

"I'm afraid this is not my most sophisticated look," Taylor said from behind him.

He turned to see her wearing a pair of bright red knee-high Wellington boots with her sundress. It wasn't the least sexy thing he'd ever seen. Not by a long shot. The stretch of bare thigh between the tops of her boots and the hem of her dress was doing something to him. Making it hard to look away. Making him think about his hand right there, slowly sliding under her skirt. "You'll be ready for mud puddles?"

"And just my luck, I don't think it's rained in weeks. Somewhere I have some sandals. And sneakers. I'm definitely not walking around in my heels from last night."

"I say that the boots are perfect for now."

"Okay, then. Let's start with the grounds and then we can come back inside."

She led him out through the front entrance to a circular driveway with a three-tiered stone fountain in the center and manicured hedges skirting the outer edges. On the other side, directly opposite the front door, was the long road leading to a stately iron gate at the estate's main entrance. "What do you plan to do with this area?"

"Aside from sprucing up, not much. I think it's nice. The study where we had wine last night is right inside, and I'm thinking that's where guests can check in."

"Okay." He was going to need some time to piece together her vision. Then he'd start lending his opinion, but only when she asked for it.

They walked down the carved limestone steps and away from the house to turn back and get a better view. The castle-like home was heavily influenced by French and English design, with turrets, leaded windows and a granite foundation covered in ivy. Roman felt like he deserved an honorary degree in architecture after his years in the hotel business. He'd read countless books on the subject, drawn to the history and the way it evolved over time.

"Thoughts on the facade?" Taylor asked.

"It's very nice."

"Do you have any suggestions on changes?"

"I need to see the whole property. But let me know if you have any ideas you want to share now."

She pursed her lips, her eyes scanning the house. "I was hoping you could tell me what to do. I can't really figure out which direction to go. Do I embrace what's already here and just make it look fresh and perfect? Or do I try to make it funky and eclectic?"

"That's the big question, isn't it? Or at least part of it." Roman knew what *he* would do with the house. In his mind, he'd already sorted it out. But he wanted to know what Taylor would come up with. On her own.

She delivered a slight scowl, which somehow managed to be cute coming from her. "That's not superhelpful."

"Give it a chance. Show me the rest of the grounds."

She started off to the side of the house. "Here's the rose garden." She pointed to a vast collection of bushes in full bloom, all situated within a tidy square, with cobbled pebble walkways and a large bronze sundial in the center. "It's nice, but a little formal for my tastes. Farther down the hill is the Japanese garden and koi pond. It's very relaxing. I think guests will love it."

"Sounds nice."

Taylor walked around to the back, following a stone pathway. "This is the main pool area, which you saw last night when we came inside. There's a second pool, behind the guest cottage, which has two bedrooms and two full baths." She pointed off into a wooded area, a good thousand yards away. "There's a tennis pavilion with four full-size courts, plus regulation bocce ball."

It all sounded quite good. Guests would certainly not get bored. "Is there anything particularly special about the property? Something perhaps that guests can't get anywhere else?"

"Well, the view up the hill from the rose garden is spectacular."

"Show me."

She led him up a grassy slope at the far right

edge of the expansive lawn, then into a wooded area, which was immaculately kept, not so much as a stray branch on the forest floor. They walked along a footpath and when they emerged on the other side, in the clearing, it was as if the whole world opened up before them. They were at a much higher elevation than Roman ever would have guessed, so you could not only see the full stretch of blue sky overhead, but also drifts of bright green trees reaching all the way down to Long Island Sound.

"On a clear day, you can see Manhattan."

"Now, this is special, Taylor. Truly."

"I'm so glad you think so. I was starting to think you were bored."

Clearly, she did not understand his process. "I'm not bored. I'm digesting the information. Taking it all in. Would you like it if I simply started mowing you over with my opinion on everything?"

"Every successful businessperson I've ever met thinks that their opinion is a gift to the whole world. They're just waiting for the right opening to give it away."

"Well, I'm not like that. Now show me the rest of the house."

Taylor seemed miffed, but Roman wasn't about to stray from what he believed to be the best course. He was a firm believer in nurturing talent, not molding it. What was the old saying? Give a man a fish and he eats for a day, teach a man to fish and he eats for a lifetime? Roman wasn't about to serve Taylor this particular fish. He wanted her to catch it on her own.

Back inside, she showed him the common areas—a dining room that could seat twenty comfortably, a full library, a formal living room with five separate conversation areas and a grand piano, several more studies including one with an impressive billiards setup, a sunny breakfast room overlooking the pool area, and even a small theater with room for twelve or so people.

"Aside from the wine cellar downstairs and the laundry room, that's pretty much everything," Taylor said, now that they were back where they started, in the kitchen. She sat on the barstool and one by one, pulled off the boots. She wiggled her toes and stretched out her legs. "I'm so happy to take those things off. They're surprisingly hot."

All he could think was that she was so hot he was surprised she wasn't on fire. "I'm glad you're more comfortable."

"Well?" She delivered a pointed stare. "Are you going to tell me what you think of the house?"

"You definitely have the start of something here. The question is what you want to do with it."

"Which is why I bid on you in the auction."

He took a seat next to her at the kitchen island. The proximity was like being seated next to her on the helicopter, when her fear and the tight quarters made closeness the only sensible option. They'd known each other for two hours then, and it was still one of his most electric memories in recent time. "I realize that. But I don't want to tamper with your vision by giving you my ideas first. It needs to be the other way around."

"Oh, no. You're the one with the vision. Not me. I'm creative, but I'm not next-level like you are. I want to do more than put nice linens on the beds and fancy soaps in the bathrooms. I want there to be a thread that ties the whole thing together. Just like you do with your properties."

"You make it sound like you've studied them."

"I told you. I've been to every single one. At least once. They're all amazing."

Roman still couldn't comprehend that she was such a fan of his life's work. "Frankly, that's unbelievable."

"It's the truth. I've been to Boston, of course. Your original hotel."

"Of course." A pang of regret went through him every time someone mentioned the Boston property. Even though it was universally loved and had launched his career, there was too much sad history associated with it.

Like a corporate brochure brought to life, she began rattling off his company's many locations, starting with San Francisco and Chicago and ending with Paris and Madrid, counting them out on her fingers as she went. "That's sixteen. I'm forgetting one."

Roman struggled to remember which property was missing, a pathetic realization when this was his business they were talking about. "Hong Kong?"

"Yes. That's it. I love them all. And all for different reasons. They each have their own flavor, their own vibe, which I think is so cool, but I still know I'm at one of your properties when I'm there. How do you do that?"

"I can't really quantify that for you, Taylor. All I can say is that I look at a property and the more time I spend there, the more it starts to reveal itself to me. I suppose it's like a sculptor working on a piece of stone. The more they chip away at it, the closer they get to the essence of what they want to express. Except that I would never compare myself to an artist."

"But you are one. You're a genius."

That word stopped him dead in his tracks. "No. I'm not. Please don't call me that."

"What? Genius?"

Each time she said it, she pried him open a little more. She made glimpses of his past seep back into his consciousness, things he'd worked hard to forget. Memories of losing his only love. His wife. Abby. And the lies that were uncovered when she was gone. "Yes. I'm asking you to not use that word. Please."

"But I don't understand. You are one. Most men would be fawning all over me for calling them that. You really take humbleness to a whole new level. It's shocking, really."

He could be fawning all over her in a heartbeat. As long as she didn't heap praise on him that he didn't deserve. For right now, he needed a break. From Taylor's beauty. From the temptation of her lips and her face and her body. Most important, a respite from this conversation. It was turning him into something he didn't want to be. "I need to go up to my room for a few minutes."

"I'm sorry. Did I offend you?"

He pivoted on the barstool in order to stand, and his back went into spasms. "Ugh…" He tried to swallow the groan of agony that burst forth from his mouth, but there was no stopping it. Reflexively, he grabbed at the pain point and arched his spine, but his muscles protested, binding up tighter as his legs went weak and he had to sit again.

"Oh, my God. Roman. Are you okay?" Taylor hopped up and planted her hands on his shoulders, peering up into his face with eyes that were wide and panicked.

He cursed his own body. It was not only in utter anguish, it was apparently capable of doing two things at once as it soaked up Taylor's touch and sent heat surging through him again. He clamped his eyes shut, if only to take her beauty out of the equation and collect himself, still perched on the edge of the seat. "I'm fine. It's just…" He had to fight to get out the words. He hated feeling weak. He hated feeling like she might be pitying him.

"You are not fine. Is it your back? Did you hurt yourself recently? Do you have an old injury? Does this happen a lot?"

Roman opened his eyes. "You ask an awful lot of questions."

"I have some experience with this. Does it feel better to sit or stand right now?"

"Either is okay. It's the in-between part that's causing problems."

"Gotcha. Then let me help you stand."

"I've got it." He didn't want to let his pride get in the way, but he also didn't like feeling like an old man. He dropped his feet to the floor and straightened, but it was a rough transition. He knew he looked hobbled.

Taylor grasped his biceps with one hand while gently sliding across his lower back with the other. "Does this hurt?"

He winced at the sensation of her touch, a cruel mix of agony and pleasure. "It doesn't feel great," he lied. Yes, there was stabbing pain, but her touch was pure magic, sending pleasurable waves of warmth through his muscles.

She moved her hand lower several inches, dangerously close to his ass. "What about this?"

"Definitely tender." *And sensitive. And amazing.*

"Here's the deal. One of my many short-lived careers was massage therapy. And we have a massage table in the gym. Let me work out these knots."

"That's pretty far outside the terms of our agreement."

"Roman. You're giving me days of business advice, *and* you brought me here in your helicopter. This is the absolute least I can do."

"Are you sure?"

"Positive. Plus, you won't be any good to me if you're stuck in a chair, or even worse, in bed. I've already seen you without your shirt, so we don't need to worry about modesty issues."

It's just that I'm not sure what will happen if you touch me like that again. "Okay."

"Come on, handsome. Let me make you feel better." Taylor took his hand and started for the hall. Roman trailed behind, feeling like he was on a ride where he had zero control. Her silky hair swung back and forth, calling for his fingers. Her bare shoulders begged for a kiss. He was electrified by her.

And he wanted to return the favor.

Five

Taylor worried she was letting her weakness for men take over. Was Roman really that bad off? Or had she invented a reason to touch him and he'd simply acquiesced? *He's in pain and you can help him. Calm down. It's fine.*

Since it was a beautiful day and the gym had a set of French doors that led to the back terrace, Taylor set up the table outside in a shady spot. It was at the far end of the pool where the warm water from the hot tub cascaded over an infinity edge and into the pool. It was a peaceful backdrop, and she tried to focus on the therapeutic benefits of sound and water, rather than the seductive ones. Roman needed to relax. And she intended to help him do that. She brought out a bottle of massage oil, and several towels, one to roll up under his ankles to relieve any pressure on his back when he was facedown. The other was to cover him up.

"Let me help you with your shirt," she said. "It can be hard to lift your arms over your head when your back is spasming."

"Oh. Sure."

She'd already seen him without a shirt. Been there, done that. She was fully prepared. But as she helped him lift it over his head and her hand brushed his chest and his forearm grazed her nipple through the thin fabric of her sundress, it felt like two ends of a circuit had been connected. Heat shot through her, jolting her awake, leaving her with a deep, unsatisfied and painful ache for him. It made zero sense that it was like this after one day of knowing him, especially since he represented her greatest professional hope. If she wasn't careful, she was going to torpedo her future by allowing these physical urges to get the better of her.

She stepped back to break free from the connection, but that only gave her a better view of him. He had the exact kind of build she loved—tall and trim and just enough definition in his shoulders and biceps to let her know that he took good care of himself. Roman was Taylor's type the way water was wet. She had every reason to feel threatened by that. On guard. But when it came to Roman, one glance at him and her fears dissolved into nothingness. They disappeared into nothing, like a wisp of smoke up a chimney. Was it his brains? His brilliance? She was desperate for the answer, and then it hit her—their time together was limited. He'd be gone by Monday. Every other guy who'd hurt her had stuck around long enough to really make it sting. But not Roman. He was going to exit her life just as quickly as he'd entered it. And that was a good thing. She hoped.

"I'm not going to be able to get to your lower back if you're wearing jeans." She cleared her throat. "Or underwear for that matter. I need access."

"Oh, really?" He cast her a narrowed glance, along with a playful arch of both eyebrows.

"If you're worried I'm trying to get into your pants, don't be. They'll already be gone."

He laughed and shook his head as he unbuttoned his pants, making her throat grow tight. "You're in charge."

Not exactly. "I promise not to look." She held up a towel and turned her head, while her pulse pounded at the base of her throat.

"Exactly how good are you at keeping promises?"

"Probably not as good as I should be."

There was the sound of a zipper, followed by silent movement she couldn't see but sensed. Possibly his clothes landing on the pool deck? "Ready."

"I need you on the table facedown. Can you get up there on your own?"

"I think so." He groaned as the table creaked.

She reflexively turned, thinking she was going to need to give him a hand, but he was already stretched out, leaving her with a full and enticing view of the naked landscape of the back half of his body. Her sights drifted over him, taking in every tempting inch. This was Roman Scott, after all, a male specimen rivaled by very few. His butt was magnificent—perfectly round and muscled with those mind-blowing flat planes at the sides of his hips. Her breath hitched in her throat, and she knew she hesitated for a moment or two too long before she draped the towel across his ass. Did he know she'd looked? And how did he feel about that?

Ridiculously, her brain told her to be professional. All hopes of that were clearly out the window. Less than twenty-four hours after meeting the man she hoped would help her build a new business and career, she'd seen him naked. How did she get herself into these situations? Again, she forced herself to take stock—the man was in physical agony and she could take that away. She'd said she would help. It would be worse to walk away now. "I'll start on your upper back and shoulders. Just to help you loosen up before I move to that more sensitive spot."

"Sounds perfect." His voice was rich and thick, making her wonder why everything about him had to be so damn sexy. It was like he had an endless supply of it.

Her hands silky and slick with massage oil, she pressed into his shoulder blades, her thumbs along the channel of his spine and her fingers spanning his upper back. His body heat zipped into her, traveling up the length of her arms, leaving behind a lasting tingle. As she curled her fingers and began kneading his muscles, she marveled at how strong and solid he was, even when his skin was impossibly smooth and touchable. She took a deep breath, hands glazing over his back, going deeper into the tissue, touching more and more of him with every caress and pass.

He unleashed a low but pleased groan. A quiet hum of relief. She was reminded of the reasons she'd pursued massage therapy in the first place—it felt good to help someone else feel better.

"Pressure okay?" she asked.

"Better than okay." He shifted on the table and rolled his neck slightly, then settled back in. "Your hands are magic."

She smiled to herself, experiencing a sense of pride she hadn't felt in so long. So much of her life lately had been about failure. It was nice to be reminded that she didn't come up short at everything. Her foray into massage had been short-lived, but it was certainly paying dividends today. "Thanks."

"Seriously. If I didn't already know you have vastly different career aspirations, I'd hire you right now to be a full-time masseuse."

"Hmm. Sounds like you've just given me a solid fallback plan."

Her hands skimmed lower, inching closer to the small of his back. Every minute brought a new level of familiarity between them, her body and his in this beautiful symbiosis that was both mesmerizing and hypnotizing.

"I'll pay you whatever you want."

All Taylor could think was that touching him was compensation enough.

She now felt he was relaxed enough for her to start work on his trouble spot, but she still proceeded with caution, using a delicate touch. "Let me know if this hurts at all." Her thumbs aligned with his lower spine, her fingers curved to meet the contours of his waist. She kneaded slowly, in a steady and rhythmic pattern, his muscles loosening and lengthening beneath her touch. "Is this okay?"

"Yes. Perfect."

Her hands glided lower, nudging the towel down bit by bit, and it felt so good to touch him and heal him, that again, instinct took over. She worked her fingers into the taut muscles at his hips, and that left her palms pushing the towel lower. He tensed. And that shook her out of the trance of the massage. She froze, her hands still spanning the lowest reaches of his back, half of his ass fully visible to her. "Too much?"

He hesitated for a moment. "More like too good."

She froze when she realized what he might be saying. "We can stop."

He hesitated to answer, leaving her with her hands on his back, the steady woosh of the waterfall in her ears and the sweet scent of summer in her nose. "I'd be an idiot to tell you to stop."

She hadn't realized she'd been holding her breath until it rushed forth from her lips. "Okay. Good. Because I was just getting somewhere." She recognized the double meaning in her words the instant they left her mouth, but she didn't regret them. She loved pushing past barriers. The danger of the unknown was a drug to her, just like Roman was.

"You are *definitely* getting to me, Taylor."

She swallowed hard, feeling as though she was inching closer to the edge of a beautiful cliff. "Funny, but I could say the same thing about you."

With his arms at his sides, his left hand was near his hips, which meant it was a whisper away from hers. He reached for her, brushing her fingers in soft and gentle circles. There was zero mistaking his intention. This was not the touch of a man who was merely showing his appreciation. This was about sex and lust. The realization made her breath catch in her throat. She wanted him. Even when she knew it was a bad idea. Even when she knew she shouldn't. She'd wanted him from the moment she laid eyes on him. And this would likely be her only chance.

Something deep inside her, an undeniable instinct, made her curl her fingers under the top of the edge of the towel, pull it away, and drop it onto the patio. There was shock in what she'd done, a nanosecond of regret, sent into rapid reverse when Roman rolled to his side and pushed up from the table to a sitting position. She couldn't help but look at his erection. It was right in front of her and she didn't need to touch him to know exactly how hard he was. He leaned down and dug his fingers into her hair, cupped her jaw and pulled her lips to his. She knew nothing other than to give in to the kiss with raw intensity, to meet his wild gesture with equal enthusiasm. She popped up onto her toes and braced herself on the table, her hands bracketing his hips. She stretched her neck to take the kiss deeper. His mouth was open, lips firm and craving, and his tongue hot and wet and fueled by pure need.

He slid off the table and stood on the stone patio, never breaking their kiss, sending Taylor's mind into a tailspin of what might come next. He answered the question by squeezing her waist, lifting her and turning to put her on the table, seated. He tugged at the straps of her sundress, pulling them down her shoulders and she silently begged him to keep going, to take off every stitch of her clothes, cover her bare skin with kisses, taste every inch, then bury himself in her. It was as if he heard her plea, his hands smoothing to her back and drawing down her zipper. He pulled down the garment to her waist, exposing her breasts to the open air. He gripped her rib cage and drew one nipple into his mouth, his tongue swirling and teasing and making her want to buck into him. It had been months and months since she'd had sex and Roman had opened the floodgates. There was no stopping this train. It had left the station.

"You are so damn sexy," he muttered, then shifted his mouth to her other breast.

"I was just thinking the same thing about you." She dug one hand into his silky hair while her other was planted on the table, letting her arch her back and give him full access to her chest. The heat and need sizzled between her legs. She needed every inch of him.

He slid one hand into the back of her dress, caressing her bare skin, while the other hand palmed her thigh, skimming up under her skirt. She bent her elbow, angling her body back farther as he reached her panties and began pulling them past one hip. She was tired of being held back by her clothes, so she turned slightly and eased back on the table. With her dress bunched up at her waist, she lifted her hips and wriggled her panties down to midthigh, with Roman doing the rest of the work and whisking them away.

"Touch me, Roman," she said, splayed out on the table before him. She was as vulnerable as could be, her nipples hard and breasts full, her clit absolutely aching for him.

He held her gaze as the midday sun crept onto her shoulder and the air was sweet and sticky with the promise of early summer. "Like this?" He dragged a single finger along the top of her thigh.

Taylor arched her back and let her knees fall open. "Keep going."

He lowered his head and kissed her softly, tracing her lower lip with his tongue as his hand drifted north to her center, his fingers spread her delicate folds and found her center. He took the kiss deeper as he rubbed in circles. Round and round, but still teasing her, amping up her need for him when his touch lightened and slowed but kept grazing her sensitive skin. He slipped a finger inside her, then two, then rested his thumb at her apex and rotated, much more firmly this time.

Taylor gasped, her mind already blurry with

pleasure. The pressure was pounding at the door, her reward already so painfully close. Roman slid his mouth from her lips to her jaw, then buried his head in her neck while his hand took her higher and higher. She stretched and reached for his cock, wrapping her fingers around his hot and hard skin. As he drove in and out of her with his hand, she stroked his full length, rolling her thumb over the tip with every pass.

He groaned his approval into her ear, nipped at the lobe, then kissed her again, this time deeper and hotter. Her body grabbed onto his hand in one last desperate attempt to stay in control, and just when she thought she couldn't take another millisecond of it, she came. She called out, her head rolling back on the table. Even with the intensity of the orgasm, she never let go of Roman, and he came right after she did, his body freezing with the release.

The second her choppy breaths grew longer and her brain started to focus again, she knew she'd made a mistake. As mind-blowing as it felt, the rushing waves of pleasure absolutely flattening her into nothing, she knew this had been such a bad idea. Where were they supposed to go from there? Back to work? She couldn't see a world in which things would happen that way. All she wanted was more of him. She needed to do this again. And again. And again. With him. What in the world had she done? She was half-naked on a massage table in front of the man she needed to make her a success.

"I am so sorry," she blurted, then scrambled off

the table. She clumsily threaded her arms back into her dress, and reached back to zip it. "I don't know what happened."

"No. No. No. I'm the one who should be sorry." He grabbed a towel from the pool deck and wrapped it around his waist, then scooped up his clothes and clutched them to his chest. His embarrassment was so clear. He wouldn't even look at her.

Taylor was desperate to fix this, to save him the humiliation and somehow salvage the working relationship she'd hoped for with him. "Let's, uh, just forget that this happened." To punctuate the stupidity of the comment, she plucked her panties from the ground and balled them up in her fist.

"Right. Yes. I think that's the smart thing to do." He still wouldn't make eye contact. Instead, he scanned everything in the surrounding area that wasn't her—plants, the flagstone beneath their feet, the trees off in the distance in the yard.

"Okay, then."

"Yes. Got it." He glanced over his shoulder. "I'm just going to go upstairs. To my room."

Taylor wanted to die, or at the very least fade into oblivion. Had she ruined absolutely everything? Again? Probably. "Please. Do whatever you need to do."

Taylor needed time to think. She needed time to recover a shred of her dignity. Roman was getting to her in ways she had feared. Either he was impossibly hot or she was ridiculously weak. Although, why choose? It was pretty clear that both things were true. And so she'd given in to attraction, and probably ruined her plans for the future.

She sought the seclusion of her bedroom. Stepping in here always felt a little strange. Since this had been her family's oldest vacation home, it didn't receive frequent decorating updates. Taylor's little hideaway remained today much as it had been when she was twenty. That was the year she dropped out of college.

Her freshman year was at Princeton, and characterized by a spate of hot guys and too little studying. She could admit now that she'd been a wild child. Although she loved her parents deeply, and they'd always encouraged her to be independent, being able to live on her own and do whatever she wanted? Well, that had proven to be too big a temptation. She'd finished the year by the skin of her teeth, and she credited her boyfriend at the time, who was one of those people who never needed to study. He knew how to do everything. He'd helped her cram for exams and write papers, and she was smitten. He'd also been sleeping with her roommate the whole time.

Heartbroken and failing, she swung in the opposite direction and transferred to Bryn Mawr, a much smaller women's college her mom had attended. She hardly made it to exams her first semester, in part because she was lonely. Eventually, she dropped out, and somehow convinced her parents that they should let her live at the summer house alone. This place became her refuge. She got a job as a virtual assistant, where she could work exclusively online, and only saw her parents occasionally. Chloe and Alexandra came to visit a few times when they were on break from school. Like most things, the virtual assistant gig didn't last. One of the clients she was handling kept erratic hours and complained about her when she didn't answer his call at 3:30 in the morning. She was fired the next day. That was actually when she started looking into massage therapy. And now after her interlude with Roman, she saw exactly where that had gotten her—back in trouble again.

Why did she have so many problems staying on track when her friends Chloe and Alex had zero trouble with it? The three of them were so alike, but Taylor felt like she was always lagging behind. Constantly playing catch-up. And now she was floundering again, desperate for advice from one or both of her best friends. She needed to talk out the Roman situation. If she didn't sort it out in her head somehow, she'd never salvage what was left of her time with him.

She called Alex, thinking that there was a chance Chloe was busy with her fiancé, Parker. "Oh, my God, Taylor. We were just about to call you. It's like you're psychic," Alex said when she answered.

If only. I could've prevented that superhot but ultimately disastrous scene by the pool. "We?"

"Yes. Chloe and Parker and I got together to talk about Little Black Book. Hold on one second. Let me put you on speaker."

"Hi, Taylor," Chloe and Parker said in unison.

Great. With Parker on the phone, Taylor could

not seek any insight from her friends with regard to Roman. That would have to wait. "Hey. Did you manage to pull Alex into your plan to take down Little Black Book?"

"Alex was easy," Parker said. "It's Chloe who's still not convinced. But I'm working on her."

"So where do I come in to all of this? Alex said you were about to call me," Taylor said.

"You're in Connecticut at your family's summer house, right?" Parker asked.

"I am."

"Do you realize that Simone Astley's estate is only eight miles away from yours?" Alex inquired.

"Sort of? I'm afraid I don't see the connection."

"I know this is going to sound a little out there, but here's the story," Chloe said. "It looks like Simone Astley was the owner of the Little Black Book. The actual diary the social media account is based on. She went to Baldwell, but her family pulled her out before she could graduate. And they never enrolled her in another school. They basically kept her under lock and key at their house."

"No one knows why," Parker followed up. "The house has been untouched since she died several years ago. The property was willed to the local historical society. They tried to refuse the gift because they can't afford the taxes, so there have been some legal tangles. Word is that the historical society did take ownership, but they plan to take the contents for preservation, then put the estate on the market. We were wondering if you could go over there and snoop around before they have a chance to empty out the house. Before anyone can hunt for clues."

Taylor could hardly believe what she was hearing. She was *not* a sleuth. "Parker, don't you have an investigator working on this?"

"I do, but she's out of the country for two weeks working with another client," Parker answered. "I'd do it myself, but Chloe and I were already targeted once by Little Black Book. We can't risk it."

"And I can?" Taylor asked.

"You're the one who said gossip isn't a big deal," Alex chimed in.

Taylor quietly grumbled. "I'm up here because I'm meeting with Roman Scott. I don't really have time to go play Nancy Drew."

"How are things with Roman?" Alex asked, sounding a bit too intrigued. "I can't believe you convinced him to go up there with you."

She was in disbelief, too. It was the one right thing she'd done in a while. "Things are good. Fine," Taylor lied.

"Is he as gruff as everyone says?"

No, actually. He's magnificent and kind and ridiculously sexy. Basically, everything I've fallen for before, except all wrapped up in one man. "He's nice enough. He can be a little difficult when we're talking about my plans for the hotel."

"And are you talking about other things?" Chloe asked with a leading tone.

Taylor was desperate to get her friends off this topic, and for that matter, off the phone. She didn't want to face this line of questioning, especially since she had zero hope of help or advice right now. "Look, do you want me to go to Simone Astley's estate or not?"

"Yes," they all said in unison.

She blew out a frustrated breath. "Fine."

"Can you go today?" Parker asked. "I'm really worried about the timeline."

Taylor looked at the clock. It was a few minutes after one o'clock. At some point, she was going to have to talk to Roman. That was if he hadn't left. She hadn't heard any helicopter rotors, so she was fairly certain he hadn't departed by air, but he was a resourceful billionaire. He could call a car and be gone in no time. "No promises, but I'll try."

"Thanks, Taylor. You're the best," Chloe said.

"Are you going to give me any idea of what I'm looking for?" Several moments of quiet played out on the other end of the line. "Are you guys still there?"

"Alex has a theory that Simone Astley was pregnant. And that's why her parents pulled her out of school," Chloe said. "So I guess you're looking for some sign that there was a baby."

Taylor swallowed hard. This all sounded so unbelievable. But at least she had a distraction since Roman helping her with her hotel plans was likely all over. "Okay. But I'm going this afternoon. I'm not going over there by myself at night."

"Call us as soon as you're done," Parker said.

"I'll try." Taylor hung up the phone and tossed it aside, flopping back on her bed and staring up at the ceiling. She had to do this favor for her friends, which meant facing Roman to explain what she was doing. As if he needed one more reason to think she was erratic and impulsive.

As luck would have it, there was a knock at her door. "Taylor?" Roman asked quietly from the hall. "Can we talk?"

She sat up in bed, ready to face her fate. "Sure. Come in."

Slowly, he opened the door, looking like everything she'd ever wanted in a man. Heat flushed her cheeks, a combination of embarrassment and desire—she still wanted him, however much she felt like a fool for what had taken place. "I'm sorry about before," he said. "I never should have let that happen."

He was sorry? She felt the responsibility was on her shoulders. Not his. "It's not your fault. The massage was my idea, and I want to apologize. It was unprofessional."

"But you were just trying to help me. I appreciate that. A lot of people would have let the business get in the way. You cared more about me as a person." He blew out a breath, seeming as though he'd been unburdened a bit by getting that out. "I'm still sorry. I haven't gotten that carried away in a long time."

She'd wondered about his romantic past, but it had been so hard to learn anything personal about him. And this certainly didn't seem like the time to pry. "Don't feel bad. I broke a big promise to myself when we were down by the pool."

"Promise?"

The rules of professionalism said that she shouldn't share this information, but maybe it would help him see that the mistake wasn't solely his. "My New Year's resolution was to stay away from men. It always ends badly for me. And then it derails the rest of my life. I'm so tired of it."

He leaned against the door casing, crossing his arms over his chest. "Did that resolution have anything to do with the ex? The one who emailed you about that photo of us?"

Taylor didn't even need to hear Ian's name to feel sick at the thought of him. "Let's just say he was the proverbial straw that broke the camel's back. And yes, that happened in December." Right before Christmas, he dumped her, saying he'd rekindled things with his old girlfriend because he felt Taylor wasn't paying him enough attention.

"So there are other bad exes before him?"

"Truly bad. Laughably bad."

"Sounds like a long story."

"It's a whole bunch of long, terrible stories."

"I'm always available to lend an ear."

Good God, he was such a kind person. She found it hard to understand why his public reputation diverged so far from his true personality. "I appreciate that, but I'll save you from the drama." She sucked in a deep breath, hoping this next part would go okay. "I'm hoping that we can move past what happened down by the pool. I'd like it if we could go back to our previous dynamic." That would require a redoubling of her efforts to keep her promise to herself, but she felt it was best to get back on course as soon as you'd veered off it.

"I can do that." He offered a small smile. "Do you want to sit down tonight and go through things? I can help you with your business plan and we can dive into the financial side."

"Actually, I would love to do that. I first need to go out for a bit to run an errand for my friends, so hopefully the timing will work out."

"What sort of errand?" He straightened and took a step into her room.

Every inch closer to her bed made her want him a little more. She imagined herself settling back on the pillows and him moving in on her, stretching out on top of her, holding her down with his body weight and kissing her until she couldn't think straight. They'd done some very sexy things downstairs, but they hadn't done everything she'd wanted. *Cut it out, Taylor.* Just to be safe, she stood and distanced herself from the bed. "It's silly. You're going to think it's ridiculous."

"Try me."

She had nothing to lose at this point. Certainly he couldn't think any less of her. "This is a bit of a long story, but there was a socialite in this part of Connecticut named Simone Astley. I need to go to her house." Taylor went on to further explain everything Chloe, Alex and Parker had told her on the phone, including the connection between Simone and the anonymous social media account that was wreaking so much havoc in people's lives. "Have you heard about Little Black Book?"

"I have. It's terrible. And I hate it. I hate everything about tabloid journalism and internet gossip."

His voice was rich with conviction, but there was a biting edge there, too. She'd noticed it yesterday, after the auction, when they'd had their first run-in with the photographers and later, when their photo had turned up on that tabloid website. She wasn't sure why exactly he had such strong feelings about it, other than the fact that a lot of people felt the way he did.

"I told my friends that I'd try to find a way into the house to see what I can discover."

"Well, you're not going by yourself."

"Don't feel like you need to come with me on the wild-goose chase."

"I want to go. I'm entirely on board with taking down Little Black Book. And you don't know what you're going to encounter when you get to that house. I can't let you go by yourself. It's completely contrary to my gentlemanly ways."

Taylor nearly cracked a joke about how he hadn't quite been a gentleman by the pool, but the truth was that she was undeniably turned on by that raw and untamed side of him. It was her catnip, only she hadn't known it. "That's really nice. Thank you. We can take one of the cars in the garage."

"Sounds good. I'll meet you downstairs?"

"Just give me five minutes to change." Taylor closed the door after Roman left, then went into her closet, finding a pair of jeans and a black T-shirt, thinking that was suitable for this little escapade. Downstairs, she found Roman waiting in the kitchen. The pool was visible from the corner of her eye, causing reverberations of everything that had happened between them, but she tried to ignore it. She couldn't keep thinking of him that way.

In the mudroom, Taylor grabbed the keys for the black Porsche SUV she most often used when she was up at the house. While she was at it, she took a pair of flashlights, just in case it was dark by the time they left. They then walked out to the six-bay garage off the circular driveway, and she entered the security code to open the door. As it rolled up and away, she saw that the Porsche was shinier than the last time she'd used it. "Oh, nice. It looks like Bruce, the caretaker, took my car in to be washed. He's so thoughtful. I'm not even sure it was dirty, but it looks great." She walked around to the driver's side. "I should probably drive since I know the way."

"That will free me up to shoot out the window at the bad guys."

She laughed. "This really is silly, isn't it?" she asked as they both got settled and fastened their seat belts.

"Honestly? It's the most fun I've had in a while. And we haven't even gone anywhere."

Taylor smiled. Roman was doing his best to make things relaxed and comfortable, and she so appreciated it. No man had so effortlessly put her at ease. Roman Scott was full of surprises. And Taylor could only hope that she'd know him long enough to experience more.

"Ready?" she asked, starting the engine.

"As I'll ever be."

She put the car in gear, then rolled along at a slow speed down the long drive, careful not to kick up too much dust from the gravel. When she took a right onto the main road she picked up the pace, and they were off on their adventure.

Six

Roman was glad for their excursion away from Taylor's estate. He could still be with her, while being distracted by their mission, which was apparently to break into a dead woman's stately old mansion.

"According to the GPS, the house should be up here on the right," Taylor said. "About another half mile." They'd been traveling for more than twenty minutes, but the roads here were twisty and not suitable for high speeds.

"You've never been there before?"

She shook her head. "No. I grew up hearing about Simone Astley, but everything people said about her was like a ghost story, so I would've been too scared to go to the house. She was old and shuttered away when I was a kid."

"What can you tell me about her?"

"All I really know is that she was an only child, never got married or had kids, and was basically locked away in that house when her mother was still alive. After her parents both died, she simply stayed there. No one ever really saw her."

"Where did the family fortune come from?"

"Shipping, I believe."

"I think it's interesting that I've never heard of her," Roman said. "I grew up outside of Boston, but I did go to prep school here in Connecticut."

"You did? I didn't know that."

"Yes. Sedgefield Academy. I'm guessing you knew guys who went there."

"Roman, are you serious? I went to Baldwell."

Roman could hardly believe what she was saying. "What are the odds? That we would attend schools so close to each other? Granted, I'm nine years older than you, but still. That's an amazing coincidence."

"Yeah. Wow. My mind is officially blown." Taylor drummed her thumbs on the steering wheel. "Anyway, the stories I heard about Simone all came from Chloe's mom. That's the real connection. Chloe's grandmother was acquaintances with Simone Astley's mother."

"Interesting."

"I think this is it." Taylor leaned over the steering wheel and peered through the windshield.

Ahead on the right was the beginning of a towering ornate black wrought iron fence anchored with square stone pillars every few hundred feet. Stretching on into the distance with no visible end, the panels of metal spires were blanketed with ivy in large patches, shielding much of the house from view. For now, all they could see was a shadowy two-story mass of gray stone hiding behind a thick stand of hardwood trees.

"Any thoughts on how we're going to get onto the property? I don't know that either of us can get over that fence," Roman said.

"Maybe we'll find an opening?"

He examined the balustrade as Taylor slowed the car and followed along it. "Keep going. There has to be a service entrance. We'll try that. It should be tucked away and hopefully easier to get through." Another few minutes and he spotted it. "Pull over here. It looks like there's a trailhead on the other side of the road. If anyone sees your car, hopefully they'll think we're hiking. Not breaking into the empty mansion."

"You make it sound like you've done this before." Taylor steered onto the shoulder.

"I'm pretty good at anticipating problems." Not all of them, though. He should have been smart enough to decline Taylor's invitation for a massage earlier. He was already fighting his attraction to her, so getting naked in her presence and letting her touch him like that? It might not have been his wisest choice. But his back was feeling much better, and he'd certainly let off some steam, so it hadn't been entirely foolish.

They got out of the car and after making sure there were no other vehicles coming, they side-stepped some knee-high weeds that had sprouted up through the gravel drive leading onto the property. The gate guarding this entrance was even taller than the fence. It had a mechanical arm on the other side, and Roman suspected it would be impossible to open from this side without a key. But then he spotted an arched wood door built into the stone pillar on the right. As he approached, a sliver of light was visible around the frame, and when he reached for the handle, he saw that the lock had been bashed with something hard, like a rock.

"I don't think we're the first people to do this." He pressed his shoulder against the door, hoping it would open, but it protested at the bottom. "Something is on the other side." With some brute force, he was able to get it open about eight inches.

"We'll just have to squeeze through." Seemingly fearless, Taylor turned and contorted her body through the opening.

Roman followed, although his larger build made it more difficult. When he stumbled through to the other side, he saw what was holding the door—a sizable pile of sandbags. "Someone did not want us coming in that way. They must have left those against the door then climbed over the top?"

"Either that or they drove out." Taylor pointed to tire ruts in the gravel. They didn't necessarily look recent, but they didn't look old, either.

The hair on the back of Roman's neck stood up. Something odd was going on here, and he wasn't sure he was eager to find out what it was. "Let's get inside and look around before it gets dark." They walked up the service road to the house, which only grew in stature the closer they got. The building appeared to be constructed of limestone, and was of neoclassical style, characterized by grand scale and symmetry. He imagined the front of the home hosted dramatic columns, built to impress all guests. For now, he and Taylor were about to go in as the servants would have—through the back door.

This time, it wasn't difficult to get in. At all. "That was easy," Taylor said as she simply turned the knob and pushed the door open.

"And that's what worries me." Roman closed it behind them. They'd entered a mudroom, with long benches and shelves. There were still coats hanging on hooks. "It's like it's frozen in time."

Taylor looked ahead, then turned back to him. "Honestly? I'm freaked out. This place is creepy. It's so quiet. And I don't care that it's the middle of the afternoon, it's dark in here."

Roman had to agree. But he was curious now. He wanted to know more. "Thirty minutes. We'll look around and then we'll go back, okay?"

"Okay. But hold my hand. I don't want to lose you."

"Deal." He reached for her, wrapping his fingers around hers. Much like their ride on the helicopter, he liked being able to comfort her. Reassure her that everything would be okay. It had been so long since he'd been able to do that, be the rock in someone's life, even if this was temporary. "Don't worry. It'll be fine."

They proceeded through a kitchen that, even though it was dated, could rival any restaurant, then into a central hall. Spoking off from that were a butler's pantry, a breakfast room and several parlors filled with furniture covered with dust cloths. It was as if someone had pressed Pause on this house. As if they planned to come back.

Next they reached the foyer, with black-and-white checkerboard marble tiles, ceilings more than thirty feet high and the largest chandelier Roman had quite possibly ever seen. A grand staircase was opposite the front door, with wood treads covered in an emerald green carpet runner that was worn in the center.

"If we're looking for evidence that someone had a baby, I'm thinking we're looking for a nursery. And that would be upstairs," Roman said.

Taylor squeezed his hand a little tighter. "Makes sense."

He switched on his flashlight and they proceeded up the stairs, then started to the left side of the upper floor to explore. But as they went from bedroom to bedroom, they were able to find no sign that a child had lived there. Like the main floor, the bedrooms were still largely furnished, filled with beds and bureaus covered in old sheets. Heavy curtains hung from the windows, while painted landscapes and the occasional still life adorned the papered walls. Roman was struck by how little warmth or personality there was in this house. There was certainly no evidence that love or family had ever lived there.

At the end of the hall, they found a library with shelves stuffed with books, so many that it would take a lifetime to consume them. Taylor dropped his hand and began reading the spines while Roman was drawn to the corner, where there sat one of the few chairs in the house that wasn't covered with a drape. It was a French bergère chair, upholstered in a blue-and-white floral fabric, with aged oak arms and legs. Next to it was a reading lamp, small side table and a stack of books that had apparently tumbled off it. Out of some bizarre need for tidiness, Roman kneeled down to straighten them, and a bundle of photos fell out of one. The pictures were of people, and they were taken in this house.

"Taylor. I found photos."

"Ooh. Let me see." She rushed over and kneeled next to him. It only took a quick glance for her to identify the first person they came across. "That's her. That's Simone Astley. I've seen pictures before." She pressed her shoulder right against Roman's and pointed to the young dark-haired woman in the photograph. She was standing in the downstairs front parlor they'd explored minutes earlier, with a sly smile on her face, like she was hiding something.

As they flipped through the other images, nearly every one featured Simone. She had been a striking beauty, with a willowy figure and piercing eyes. A few also featured a dour older woman, presumably her mother. The most peculiar was one taken at

Christmas. It was of Simone standing next to the holiday tree, holding an unusually large wrapped gift. It was so big that it obscured her entire midsection.

"Oh, my God. She's hiding a baby bump." Taylor pointed to the spot right beneath Simone's bustline, where a slight curve was present. "Also, her face is pudgier than in any of the other pictures. I think she's pregnant."

Roman was no expert on the subject, but he had noticed that his sister-in-law Fiona's face had become fuller during her pregnancies. "I think you might be right."

"But we haven't seen a single thing in this house that suggests a child ever lived here. Everything is so stuffy and overly formal," Taylor said.

"I have two thoughts on that. I mean, a child would eventually grow up, right? So we might not end up finding anything. But I also know there's a lot we haven't explored yet. Perhaps we should keep looking."

Taylor nodded eagerly as it seemed that the gears in her head were now turning. "Let me snap some pictures of these on my phone. I don't feel right taking them, but they could be important."

Roman helped Taylor capture both the front and back of each photo, as most contained dates on the reverse side. Then they went on to explore the rest of the top floor, but came up with nothing. It seemed as though they'd hit a dead end, but Roman got an idea. "We haven't looked through the servants' quarters yet."

Taylor glanced out one of the dingy windows. "It's really getting overcast outside. I'm wondering if we're in for bad weather. I don't want to be stuck in this house in the rain."

"One quick look, then we're out of here."

"I suppose it's worth a shot." They headed back to the first floor, wound their way down the main hall and through the kitchen until they found the back staircase. Taylor shined her flashlight into the claustrophobic passageway. "You have to go first, Roman. There's no way I can lead the way."

He wasn't feeling considerably more brave than she was, but he did again feel the need to protect her. "Of course." Step by step, they descended into the basement. Musty smells filled his nose, but Taylor clung to his shoulder, staying right behind him and keeping herself nearly plastered against his back. He loved this closeness with her, even though it was once again stirring things up in him that he hadn't faced in quite some time.

At the bottom of the staircase, they were confronted by a narrow corridor with closed doors on both sides, low ceilings and no natural light. One by one, zigzagging across the hall, he opened each door and shined his flashlight into the tiny Spartan spaces. If a child had lived down here, there was certainly no sign of them.

"This is pointless," Taylor said, sputtering. "It's dirty and dusty down here and we aren't discovering anything other than the fact that people used to treat their servants like crap. Who would want to live down here? Not me, that's for sure."

"Two more rooms. Then we're done." He opened the next door. Something scurried across his feet. He jumped.

Taylor screamed. "Oh, my God! A rat!" She practically leaped into his arms, flattening him against the wall while the beam of her flashlight darted up and down the hall. "Where did it go? Where did it go?"

Roman couldn't help it. He laughed and pulled her closer. She turned and her face was mere inches from his. She was breathing hard, lips slack with surprise. The tightness he'd experienced in his hips when she started the massage had returned with a vengeance. But he welcomed it now. He was tired of fighting his own body. Tired of ignoring his own desires. "I'm sure you scared the hell out of whatever that was."

She swatted at his shoulder, but let out a breathy chuckle. "It's not funny."

"Hey. You're laughing, too."

"You must think I'm a total wimp. Between the helicopter and this, I probably seem like a scaredy-cat."

He shook his head slowly from side to side, not taking his sights off her in the low light. "We're all capable of being fragile, Taylor."

"I never said fragile. That makes me sound completely pathetic."

"Okay. How about if I simply call you human?"

"That's better."

"Sort of like me earlier today."

"We don't have to talk about it."

He realized that was true. But he liked Taylor a great deal and he didn't want there to be things left unsaid between them. If nothing else, he wanted her to appreciate that he was drawn to her. He was about to launch into an explanation and a request to kiss her, but Taylor interrupted him with a gasp.

"Roman! Look!" She broke free from his arms, and stepped into the room the creature had just escaped. A beam of light crawled up the wall, revealing a poster with the ABCs on it. In the corner was a tiny bed. Too big for a baby. Too small for a teen.

"Huh," he said. "I guess this means we found it. But I'm not sure I know what this means."

Taylor blew out a frustrated breath through her nose. Her shoulders dropped. "Yeah. Me neither." She pulled out her phone and snapped a few pictures. "I guess this will have to do for now. Can we please get out of here?"

Roman wanted nothing more. "Yes. Let's go."

It started to rain as Taylor drove back to the house. The windshield wipers swished back and forth, the sky grew darker and she tried to stay focused on the road. Her mind was racing after the visit to Simone Astley's estate. It felt as though all they'd unearthed were a lot of questions and very few answers.

The same could be said of Roman and her. They'd had their hot encounter at the pool that morning, then they'd decided to forget that it ever happened.

Only that resolution didn't last very long. Shortly after, they were holding hands in an abandoned old mansion, and she eventually landed in his arms when something scurried across the room. She had come *this* close to kissing him then. There was some sort of magnet between them, drawing her in. If it hadn't been such a creepy setting, she would have let her lips land on his and let things go wherever they chose to go. For now, all she wanted was to get home, where they could be alone and safe. And now they were almost there.

She pulled her car into the garage and turned off the engine. They both climbed out then stood at the open door as sheets of rain came down before them. "Unfortunately, this is one of the downsides of this house. We're going to have to make a run for it."

He dismissed it with a wave of his hand. "Just some water. No big deal. I'll race you." Before she could reply, Roman tore off across the circular drive and headed for the front door. The only problem? Taylor did not have a key.

"Roman!" she yelled. "Go that way!" she directed him by pointing frantically toward the backyard.

"What?" he yelled back, squinting at her as the rain doused him.

"Go to the back door. I don't have the key for the front! And there's no keypad."

"Oh! Okay!" He made a run for it and Taylor chased behind, the two of them racing down the pathway through the side yard and around to the back of the house until they reached the mudroom door.

They squeezed themselves under the small gabled roof over this entry, which was only partially protecting them from the rain, which was now coming down sideways. With wet hands, Taylor fumbled with the keypad, her fingers sliding off the buttons. Water dripped down her nose while all of this proximity to Roman was making her feel a little reckless again. His chest was pressed against her back, his hand on her arm as he impatiently watched over her shoulder. When she finally got the code right and the lock turned, they stumbled inside together and Taylor closed the door behind them, muffling the sound of the rain.

"I'm drenched," Roman said. "These shoes are in rough shape." He leaned over and untied his running shoes, then toed them off, making Taylor stifle a sigh of appreciation for his ass in those jeans.

"Mine, too," Taylor said, kicking off the sneakers she'd found in her closet upstairs earlier.

"I guess we shouldn't track all of this water into the house, huh?" He began unbuttoning his shirt.

She had a feeling where he was going with this, and it made her question her priorities again. The smart thing to do would be to keep Roman in the professional friend zone. But she was having a very hard time resisting him, especially when they were all alone, with absolute privacy. "It would just make a big mess. We wouldn't want to do that." Impulsively, she whipped off her black T-shirt, then soaked up the moment when he looked at her in her lacy black bra.

His eyes went dark with desire as he rolled his

shoulders out of his shirt. She loved his chest so much, it was hard to peel her sights away, but she was too focused on his face right now. The way his lips parted. The air was charged with anticipation. Was he thinking what she was thinking? She hoped to hell he was. She didn't want to talk to Roman. She didn't want to flirt or toy around with their attraction. What they'd shared that morning had been amazing, but it wasn't everything she'd wanted.

"Better?" He dropped his chin, stepping closer, chipping away at her patience with a fiery flash of his eyes. He gripped her elbow and electricity ran through her. Finally, touching. Someone had broken the barrier.

Taylor was a little too aware of her pounding heartbeat and the sway of her body as she stood before him in her jeans and bra. "My pants are stuck to me. I think I'm going to have to peel them off."

"I can help with that." A clever smile crossed his lips and it created such an immediate blip of happiness in her heart that she wondered how she'd ever made it through a day of her life without him.

"Okay."

He reached down and unbuttoned her jeans, his damp hands a bit cold against the warm skin of her bare belly. As he drew down the zipper, she placed her hands on his shoulders and he took that as an invitation to kiss her neck as he wriggled the pants down past her hips, and she stomped her way out of them, leaving them in a pile. That brief brush of his lips only made her hungry for more, so she returned the favor with his jeans, while he combed his fingers through her damp hair.

As soon as his pants met the same fate as hers, she closed her eyes and went for it, smashing her lips against his in a kiss that made her feel like she was floating. There was no hesitation when he kissed her back, his tongue seeking hers and exploring her mouth. Every inch of her body delighted in his kiss, even the parts that were so far away from his lips. He was that good at it. She slid her forearms up onto his shoulders and dug her fingers into the thick hair at his nape. He slid his warm lips to her jaw and then her neck again. He reached the sensitive spot below her ear and for a moment, she thought she might come just from that. He wound his arms tightly around her, pulling her against his frame and nearly lifting her from her feet.

"Tell me you don't want this," Roman said, breathless, his face buried in her neck.

"I won't lie to you. I want this. More than anything right now."

"Good. Because I do, too." He reached behind her and unhooked her bra, then dragged the straps down her arms. His vision sank lower. "You're stunning, Taylor. You deserve everything you want." He gripped her rib cage with both hands, his thumbs caressing the sensitive underside of her breasts. The air in the room was cool against her overheated skin, making her nipples tighten. Or maybe that was the anticipation of what he was about to do as he lowered his head and sucked one of the tight buds between his lips.

The gasp that came out of her sounded like pressure being relieved, and in many ways it was exactly that. No, this wasn't what she'd planned on, nor was it what she'd promised herself. But in the moment, it was the only thing that made sense and the only thing she wanted. She knocked her head back when he switched to the other breast, sending ribbons of needs through her. "I want you, Roman."

"Upstairs," he muttered, sweeping her into his arms. He held her close against him as he wound his way through the kitchen and then to the stairs.

"My room." She clung to his neck and turned her face into his chest, breathing in his warm and masculine smell. The journey to her bedroom seemed like it took forever, but that was the anticipation speaking, teetering on the brink of having what she wanted.

When they reached their destination, her room with the generous king-size bed and the windows overlooking the backyard, she was ready to get lost in him. He set her down on the mattress, smiling. The soft evening light showed off the tempting contours of his shoulders and abs. She shifted to her knees and spread her hands across his firm chest, warming her hands against his skin. But touching him wasn't enough. She was desperate to have his mouth on hers again. And when she kissed him, he returned it with such force that she was knocked back, but she grabbed his biceps at the exact right time and they fell onto the bed together in a heap.

She dipped her fingers beneath the waistband of his black boxer briefs, tugging them down his hips. Her kissed her again as she wrapped her hand around his length, and she swallowed the groan that he made into her mouth. He urged her to stretch out on the bed, then kissed her bare stomach, before sitting back on his knees. He curled his fingers around the top edge of her panties and pulled them down, all while he teased her with his eyes, reminding her of how good it was going to feel when he touched her. Their gazes connected as his fingers met her apex and he rocked his hand back and forth, leaving her feeling nothing less than utterly wanted and desired. Every bit of misery from her past faded away into the recesses of her mind. Maybe it wasn't that men were her downfall. Maybe it was that not all men were Roman.

The pressure was already building, but she wanted everything she hadn't had down by the pool. "I want you inside me."

He dropped his head again and pressed open-mouthed kisses to her lower belly. "Do you have a condom?"

"Yes." She rolled to her stomach and pulled open the drawer of the bedside table, plucking one from the box. Meanwhile, Roman dragged his luscious mouth along her spine. She rolled to her back. "Do you want me to put it on?"

"Yes."

He stretched on the bed next to her, and she could only think that she was an incredibly lucky woman.

He was too handsome for words. She returned the favor of kisses on the belly, then rolled on the condom. When she raised her head and their gazes connected, it looked as though he was ready to set her on fire. And she hoped that would be exactly what would happen.

Roman reached for her shoulders and gently flipped her to her back, hovering over her, leaving her feeling sexy and desired. She arched her back as he positioned himself between her legs and drove inside, then she tilted her hips to meet him and let him sink as far into her as he cared to go. Her brain was a whirlwind of thoughts, many of them only fragments and ideas, but the clearest one was this: she'd thought he'd feel amazing. And she'd undersold it by a lot.

He rolled his hips with every thrust, expertly pushing her toward her peak. The pressure was coiling in her belly, gathering in her thighs, making her breaths tight and short. Her fingers dug into his muscled back, then she dragged them up, hoping she would leave at least a bit of a mark on him. She wrapped her legs around him as he kissed her long and deep, hoping she was sending the right message. She didn't want him anywhere else. And she wanted him to be kissing her when he came. She wanted that instant of connection, especially when she knew there was a good chance that Roman Scott would not become a fixture in her life. This was to capture memories. Things she could cling to as she stared down her future.

She was close, and it felt like Roman was, too.

Every pass he made was deeper and longer, but she also felt the tension radiating from his hips, as if he was having to work hard to keep his orgasm at bay. Every sound he made was breathless and desperate, reminding her that no matter what happened, there was electricity between them and at least they'd had a chance to explore it. The peak was within reach and she was ready to claim it, even when she wasn't ready for this to be over. Her body was clutching and releasing, getting closer and closer, and then finally the wave came over her, pulling her under into a world of bliss and pleasure. Roman gave way mere seconds later, confirming that he'd been holding out for her. As she pulled his hips closer with the back of her legs, he froze and called out into her neck. A smile crossed her lips, then he collapsed at her side. Being with Roman was sheer bliss. If she'd had to break her rule, she'd definitely done it with the right man.

Seven

This time when Roman woke, there was no stabbing pain in his back, but rather a beautiful woman in bed next to him. Last night with Taylor had been absolutely magnificent. They'd taken their time with each other. The pool was hot, but last night? It was far more satisfying.

She was asleep in the crook of his arm, her silky hair so soft against his skin. He didn't want to wake her, so he carefully reached for his phone, which was on the nightstand on his side of the bed. He figured he'd scroll through some emails, maybe type out a one-handed answer or two if there was anything urgent, and then enjoy the rest of his Sunday with Taylor, talking about her business and helping her pull together her vision.

But the first thing he was greeted by, a text from his brother, Derrick, made him wish he'd never thought to try to catch up on work.

Structural engineer needs more time. Could delay us a month. Trying not to freak out.

Roman and Derrick were in the early stages of their first joint project, a Scott hotel in Manhattan. Hotels were not Derrick's area of expertise, but he did specialize in real estate development and had come across a one-of-a-kind historic building for sale on Pearl Street in the financial district. Derrick knew the seller, Roman had been searching for the perfect site for the next jewel in his empire and a partnership was born. Derrick and Roman were hypercompetitive when they were young, but as they'd grown older and closer, they learned it was better to be supportive. That process started when Roman lost his wife years ago.

I'm sorry, Roman replied. What can I do?

Not sure. Fiona is not happy.

Roman had worried about that. Derrick and Fiona did extremely well for themselves, but with a second child on the way, they'd recently moved into a much larger and more expensive apartment. After a whole lot of renovations, most going over budget, it had been a stretch for Derrick to put in his half for the hotel property. Fiona, eight months pregnant, was understandably concerned about finances. Derrick had several other large projects in the works and they were overextended.

I can always float you if you need help.

We've talked about this. No. Derrick had refused to take so much as a penny from Roman. He was too proud.

Would it help if I talk to her?

Can you come today? Assure her we'll be okay?

Roman couldn't say no to his brother, but he also didn't want to end his time with Taylor. He was due to leave tomorrow morning and had so been looking forward to their day together. I'll see. Maybe dinner?

That would help me a ton.

Okay. More soon.

Roman cast aside his phone, and Taylor stirred in his arms. She hummed and smoothed her hand over his chest, curling into him and wrapping her arm around his waist. As much as he loved every second of it, this closeness left him unsettled. He'd had plenty of sex over the years, but it had been a long time since he'd slept in the same bed as a woman, and cuddled the next morning. Even though it came naturally, he still felt out of practice. And he worried about what Taylor expected from him now. She'd made it clear at the beginning that she didn't want *him*, she wanted his help. Well, now she had both, at least for a few more hours.

"Are you up?" she asked.

"Sort of. I was checking my phone."

"Uh-oh. I don't like that tone in your voice." How had she figured him out so quickly?

"There's a chance I might have to leave early."

"Of course. You should do what you have to do." That answer had come a little too quick. Was she thinking that it was an excuse?

"My brother needs my help."

"Is something wrong?"

"I think I mentioned that he and I are partnering on a project. It's a new Scott hotel. We're running into a few hiccups."

"I get it. It's your project and your family. That's more important."

He sighed. "It's not that it's more important. It's just different. And hard for me to say no. I'm really sorry. I don't want to disappoint you."

"You don't owe me anything." She rolled away from him, climbed out of bed and grabbed her robe from the back of the bathroom door. He loved watching every second of her traipsing around her room naked, and he equally disliked the moment when she took away that luscious view. "We both knew that you coming up here for the weekend was well outside the parameters of what I paid for at the auction."

He sat up in bed and tossed back the covers, rounding to her side of the bed. "Taylor. There were no real parameters. And don't you think things have gone beyond that at this point?"

"It was one night."

Why did it sting to have her make it sound so insignificant? "A pretty amazing one." And the first he'd shared with a woman in years.

"It doesn't mean you're indebted to me. Given my track record, I would hope that you'd understand why I would push for a no-promises approach."

"Of course." He wasn't quite sure how this had gone south so quickly, but he reminded himself that he and Taylor didn't really know each other that well. What might have seemed perfect at first, perhaps didn't have much staying power. "Don't worry. I'm not the guy who's going to ask for something you aren't prepared to give. Especially since I'm not able to give those things, either."

For a few unsteady heartbeats, she just stared at him, blinking. "Then that works perfectly." She breezed past him, opened the bedroom door and started down the hall.

He had to follow her. Even though he was still naked. "Taylor. Come on. Are you mad?"

"Of course not. Everything's great. I'm going to make coffee. Find some clothes and join me."

He grumbled under his breath. It was moments like this that made him so hesitant to get involved with any woman, no matter how beguiling she might be. Relationships were hard work. Even when there weren't any surface expectations, it was easy for either party to be disappointed.

He grabbed his clothes from Taylor's room, brought them to his own, took a quick shower and dressed in jeans and a dress shirt with the sleeves rolled up. When he got downstairs to the kitchen, Taylor was working on her laptop at the island again, her back to him. Part of him felt as though it would be fine to walk up behind her, place his hands on her hips and kiss her neck. But one could argue that they'd gotten too familiar too fast. And maybe it would be better for everyone if he pulled back a bit. It wasn't like he and Taylor were going to fall in love. Or even start a relationship. This had been a fun weekend together. One night, as she'd said. It was time to start acting accordingly.

"Bruce dropped off a box of breakfast pastries from the bakery in town," she said.

"He left it while we were sleeping?" Roman was accustomed to the presence of staff in his life, but something about that was unsettling. They hadn't actually laid eyes on Bruce while they were here. He was invisible. "Does that seem odd to you?"

"No. He does that sort of thing all the time. It's the reason my parents love him."

He poured himself a cup of coffee and leaned back against the countertop, facing her. He wasn't hungry. He wasn't sure what he was anymore, other than feeling like it was time for him to move along. "Will you be upset if I leave early?"

She pursed her lips and closed her laptop. "Of

course not. Do whatever you need to do, Roman. But I would like it if we could squeeze in at least a little bit of work before you go. Your business needs to move forward, but so does mine. I'd like to have your input while you're still here, if you're still willing to give it."

Okay, then. So this really was about nothing more than business. At least Roman knew where he stood. "Sure. Why don't you get dressed and we'll run through everything we didn't get to yesterday." He stopped short of reminding her that part of the reason they hadn't gone through much of her to-do list was that they'd been off running around Simone Astley's estate yesterday afternoon.

"Good. I start interviewing contractors this week. So time is of the essence."

"This week?" Her timeline surprised him. "Doesn't that seem a little premature?"

"I told you I was moving forward right away. I think I mentioned that the first time we talked. I don't want to put my future on hold anymore. I feel like I've been treading water forever."

"Got it. Message received."

"I'll put my hair in a ponytail and throw on a pair of jeans. I'll be right back." Taylor hopped off the barstool and padded out of the kitchen.

Roman sighed and took another sip of coffee, then texted his brother again. Looks like I'll definitely be able to come for dinner. 6?

Perfect. Thank you.

This is better, he told himself. He could fulfill his promise to Taylor and make his brother and sister-in-law happy. It wasn't everything he wanted, but it was a good compromise. He texted to request the helicopter pick him up late afternoon, then tucked his phone back into his pocket.

Taylor returned a few minutes later and took a seat at the island again, opening up her laptop. "Can we talk about marketing? And look at the numbers?"

"It's early for marketing. That needs to come later. You need a name. You need to get a sense of the scope of work. And honestly, none of that can come until you have your fully realized vision of the property."

"This is why I asked for your help. I need you to help me come up with a vision. You're the genius. Not me."

"Please don't…" He pinched the bridge of his nose. Every time the word left her lips, he bristled. He didn't deserve that label. And the only other person who'd ever uttered it to him had used it to manipulate him and rip his heart out. "Please don't call me that."

"I don't understand your false modesty. And you're being so dramatic about it."

It took enormous effort to tamp down the anger bubbling up inside him. "It's very real. I don't want you to use that word because my wife used to call me that." He'd expected to regret telling her that. That information unlocked painful memories, and he kept them locked away in his head for a reason.

"You're married?" Her eyes widened with shock. She popped up from the barstool and tossed her hands into the air in dramatic fashion. "Oh, this is just brilliant. I get involved with a guy who's married? And how did I not know this? I researched you for hours and there's zero information about your past other than your brother and parents. How long have you been married?"

"I was, past tense. It lasted for two weeks. Fourteen years ago. And she's dead."

Her entire face fell. "Oh, my God. Roman. I'm so sorry. What happened?"

He hated seeing the pity on her face. He hated this topic. He hated everything about this conversation. "I don't care to relive it. In fact, I won't relive it."

"I'm just confused. How was I not able to find out anything about this?"

Everything in his body was telling him to run. His palms were getting clammy. His pulse was erratic, racing then slowing down. He took a sip of his coffee and turned his back to her, looking out on the yard. The landing spot for the helicopter was right there, and he wished he could leave now. He and Taylor had managed to have some fun, but he wasn't capable of something like this. He wasn't a bare-your-soul-over-a-cup-of-coffee sort of man. "You don't know about it because I never wanted anyone to know about it. So I had my past scrubbed. I had it erased."

"That's not possible."

"For a price, you can make a lot of things disappear." *Like a marriage. Secret identities. Lies.*

"What was her name? What was she like?" She stepped closer, making him even more fearful of her questions.

It struck him how cruel this all was. He liked to tell himself that he'd put that chapter behind him, but it was still very present. It clung to him, unwilling to let go. It was the reason he couldn't open up to Taylor. It was the reason he lived such a solitary existence. "I'm leaving in a few hours. If you want my help, now is the time."

"You're changing the subject."

"Yes, I am. If you want to talk about your project, we can."

Taylor looked utterly bewildered, and he didn't blame her. "I do want your help."

"As long as you stop putting me on a pedestal I don't belong on, we can get some actual work done."

She eased back into her seat at the barstool and returned her sights to her laptop. "Fine. I'll stop having generous thoughts about you."

"That's not what I'm asking, Taylor, okay? All I'm saying is that you seem to hold me in such esteem, and I'm not sure I'm entitled to it. Yes, I have been successful, but all of that is contingent on a lot of things, the biggest of which are timing and luck. And since you can control neither of those, I want you to focus on your vision of what you want to do. Don't replicate what I've done. Carve out your own niche. Your own ideas."

"What if I don't have a vision?"

"You already had the idea to turn this property

into something more than it is, so you do. And I can see that you care about it a great deal. So let go of your preconceived ideas of what will make you successful, and instead focus on what you want this project to be. Tap into your own instincts and follow your heart."

"Every time I've done that, I've been a complete failure. So this time, I need the help of an expert. Just tell me what to do and I'll do it."

"Everyone has false starts, Taylor. Failures. If you want to be in this business, you're going to have to stand on your own two feet. Hone your vision and zero in on it. Not everything can be a collaboration." It probably seemed like he was lecturing her, but she needed to hear these things.

"But I love collaborating with the right person. That's the entire reason I wanted your help in the first place."

His phone beeped with a text. Needing a respite from the frustration of the conversation, he pulled it out of his pocket to look. When he saw the message, his blood ran cold. The sandbags were there for a reason. Stay away or I'll share the secret you worry about most. His mind immediately flew to his wife, Abby, and everything he and Derrick had worked so hard to hide. These things might not destroy him or his business, but they would do serious damage. He had too much to lose. "We made a mistake when we went to Simone Astley's house."

"What?"

Before he could hand over his phone, he saw her

screen light up from its place on the kitchen island. She glanced at it. "Sandbags? Did you get the same message?"

They exchanged devices. They'd received identical messages.

"It has to be Little Black Book, doesn't it?" he asked.

"I don't know who else it could be. This is what happened to Chloe and Parker when they started snooping."

"Little Black Book was spying on us when we were there? That's not that far away. They could be watching us right now?" He marched over to one of the French doors leading to the patio, opened it and rushed outside. "Have you ever had the house searched for hidden cameras?" He scanned the roofline, looking for any evidence of that. He knew he sounded like he was losing his mind, but he *was* losing his mind. This feeling of having his privacy violated hit far too close to home. His heart was pounding so hard and fast that he was starting to sweat. What had he gotten himself into? Why had he allowed himself to be swayed by a beautiful face and some flattery? He was no genius. Far from it. He never should've agreed to the bachelor auction. He never should've pushed Taylor into the back of his limo. He never should've come up here in the first place.

"I don't know, Roman. Anyone could spy on us here or at the Astley estate. I don't think it would be hard. A drone alone would be enough and those are not expensive."

"You don't understand. I have things I do not want anyone to know. If those details of my life came out, my business could be ruined. Banks won't want to work with me. Investors. People will stop staying at my properties. These things can blow up quickly. It could be a complete disaster." He turned to Taylor, who was standing in the doorway from the kitchen. "And the same thing could happen to you. These are not the circumstances under which you should be starting a business. We need to stamp this out before it turns into anything." He walked over to her and took his phone from her. He typed out a reply.

Don't worry. We didn't see a thing.

"What did you say?"

"That we didn't see anything."

"But we did see something."

"Taylor. Don't say that. You need to take this seriously. This could be very bad."

She grimaced, seeming annoyed. "I don't have any secrets."

"Everyone has secrets."

"Not me. I'm a very sad open book. So I'm not worried about it."

"What about what happened out by the pool yesterday? That's a secret." His mind began to make leaps he didn't want it to. What if someone had been watching? What if they'd been watching this whole weekend? What if they'd had cameras?

"I can't undo anything we did this weekend. But I'm starting to wish that I could."

That was all he needed to hear. This was a mistake. "I need to pack my bag. I'm going to get back to the city. My brother. My work. And I think you should do the same. I'm not sure it's safe for you to be up here. Especially all by yourself."

"I won't stop you, Roman. You do what you have to do. But I'm going to do what I have to do. My future is here. It's not in the city. I'm not leaving."

Taylor was so mad at herself, and the situation, that she couldn't stand outside and watch when the helicopter whisked Roman away. Instead she stood in the kitchen and only allowed herself to wait until they safely cleared the trees. She'd endured this many times—the moment when a man left. They all walked away from her at some point. It shouldn't sting so much. She should be used to it. On some level she was, but that didn't make it any easier to endure. It didn't mean she was any less likely to take the whole thing personally. Needing distance and a bit of numbing, she left the window and her view of the backyard, grabbed the first bottle of red wine she could find, poured herself a glass and wandered into the study.

Why did I have to go and have sex with Roman? she asked herself as she curled up in one of the chairs. Of course things had devolved into a mess of misunderstandings. That was what always happened to her. And then she was stuck feeling the way she felt right now—lost and foolish. Just like she had after every job or career failure. *Virtual assistant. Massage therapist. Fashion buyer.* Just like she had every time some guy broke her heart. *Ian. Malik. Bradley.* Those lists went on and on, but they'd always been separate before today. Now her failings in her personal life had negatively impacted her career prospects. *Great job, Taylor.*

She'd known all along that it was a bad idea to let romance and business intermingle, although one could argue that what she'd enjoyed with Roman was not romance, but instead merely a case of lust unleashed. Yes, there had been moments when she'd felt more than that, but that was her tendency, to get caught up in it all. To get swept away by a man. Any ooey-gooey feelings she'd had were surely one-sided. Roman was a man with the world at his feet. He'd even lost his patience with her when they'd talked about her project, too frustrated by her inability to rise to his level. He was in a different league. And the sooner she resigned herself to that fact, the better.

The one thing she couldn't stop thinking about was the fact that he'd been married. *Married.* How had she missed that when she'd done her research? She wondered what his wife had been like. And what their relationship was like. Was she the love of his life? Were they unbelievably happy together? Was that the reason he was known for being so closed off? She imagined a relationship that was pretty close to perfect, just like Roman. Something so idyllic that he couldn't bring himself to talk about it. If Taylor had been in the same situation, hopelessly in love then losing that person after two weeks or marriage? She wasn't sure she'd be able to pick herself up off the floor ever again.

"Stop thinking about him. You're tormenting yourself," she muttered. Of course, she knew the best cure for that—a good chat with Alex or Chloe. She'd needed that yesterday, but the timing had been all wrong. Maybe she could get it now.

She called Alex, assuming again that Chloe would be with Parker. Alex answered after only one ring. "Taylor, did you go?"

"Hello to you, too."

"You told us that you were going to call us after you went to Simone Astley's house, but you didn't. I was worried."

"If you were worried, why didn't you call?"

"I wasn't *worried*, worried. Just concerned. I never worry too much about you, Taylor. You always seem to figure things out. Plus, my brother invited me over and, um, Ryder was there. So I went."

Ryder was Alex's brother's best friend and business partner. Alex had been fighting sexual tension with him for years, but Ryder was the sort of guy who put his friendship and business with her brother first. So even though they'd kissed a few times, nothing ever came of it. "Any more secret kissing?"

"No. It was annoyingly platonic."

"Sorry. I know that's got to be frustrating."

"It is what it is."

"You know what? I kind of hate that expression." Even though she'd said the same thing to Roman, it struck her as entirely too fatalistic. Some things could be changed.

"But it's the truth. There's nothing I can do about my situation with Ryder. His friendship with my brother means too much to him. End of story."

"I'm sorry." Taylor sighed.

"Is everything okay with you? Is Roman Scott still there? I can't believe you convinced him to go to Connecticut with you. What have you guys been doing? Talking about business?"

Normally, Taylor would have zero reservations about spilling her guts to Alex, but something told her to keep the personal details to herself. Part of it was embarrassment. She was disappointed in herself for having crossed that line with Roman, and she knew that Alex would only ask her why she continued to self-sabotage. "We talked a fair amount about the hotel, but I'm not sure I got much more than a vote of confidence from him. He thinks it's a good idea, but he didn't really offer any concrete advice. He said that I can't get started until I have a solid vision for what it's going to be." She looked around the room. Maybe it was that she was surrounded by too many of her familial things. Perhaps it felt too tethered to the past while she was trying so hard to look forward. "He said that I need to come up with the ideas on my own. That I can't always be seeking input and collaboration from others."

"That's the stupidest thing I've ever heard," Alex said. "That's what architects and interior designers are for. Not everyone can come up with a brilliant idea. Or see the true potential of something. Working with experts will help you see possibilities that you never even dreamed of. Then you can put your own stamp on it."

That was what she'd hoped to get from Roman, but it hadn't quite played out that way. "You know what? You're right. I start interviewing contractors tomorrow, which is a step in the right direction toward getting the house in shape. I feel like I can handle the interior design stuff on my own."

"What about an architect? If you don't have anyone specific in mind, I'm sure my brother would do it. And Ryder is brilliant. I'm sure either of them would love to help you."

Funny, but somehow Daniel and Ryder had never occurred to Taylor, perhaps because they were based in the city. One of them might just be perfect. Their firm had started in ultrahigh-end residential architecture, then branched out into commercial in the last few years. They had experience in both spheres. Plus, she'd known them both for years and trusted them. Trust was important right now, since she still felt so unsure of herself. "Alex. Why didn't I think of that? You are a genius."

She laughed. "If you say so."

Apparently not everyone hated it when that word was directed at them. "Either of them could be perfect. Do you think they're available?"

"I don't know, but I can reach out and get one of them to call you."

"Maybe start with Ryder. It'll give you a chance to talk to him."

"Don't bother with matchmaking, Taylor. I need to stop barking up that tree. Ryder and I are never going to be a couple. The sooner I resign myself to that, the better."

Just then, another call beeped in on the line. Taylor pulled her phone from her ear and glanced at the screen. "Chloe's calling on the other line."

"Conference her in. She and Parker and her mom were going over wedding plans tonight. I want to hear what they decided on."

"Okay. Hold on one second." Taylor put Alex on hold, and answered Chloe's call, then merged the two. "Are you both there?"

"I'm here," Chloe said.

"Me too," Alex answered. "Chloe, we want to hear all about the wedding. What did you decide about a venue? And have you picked a date?"

"Funny that you should ask because that's actually why I was calling Taylor."

Taylor was surprised to hear that she had anything to do with this. She'd already told Chloe that she'd help with anything, but there had been zero requests for her assistance. She assumed it was because Chloe was kind of a control freak and reluctant to delegate. "What do you need? I told you that I'm happy to help."

"Well, I wanted to talk to you about using your house as the venue. The Connecticut house."

"Wait. Seriously?" Taylor had only had a few seconds to wrap her head around this, but her immediate reaction was that it was going to throw a wrench in the start of her hotel plans.

"Yes. And I'm sure you're thinking this will be a nightmare, but hear me out." Chloe had somehow managed to anticipate Taylor's reaction.

"I'm listening."

"Parker and I don't want to spend a year or more planning a wedding. We know that the longer we take, the bigger it's going to get. More people vying for invites. My mom getting more ideas about things like centerpieces and bridesmaid favors and color coordinating everything. So we're thinking that we should just get married at the end of the summer. And since the really great venues are booked way in advance, we were thinking your place. It will give you a chance to show off the house and you can present the plans for the new hotel. It could let you build some buzz."

Taylor let that idea tumble around in her head. It might end up being quite good. It would let Taylor get a real taste for hospitality on a larger scale, and buzz among their social circles would be key in an effective launch of the property. But there were a few potential hiccups. "I do worry that I'm not sure the house is ready for that many guests. And I would have to hire people."

"The only people staying in the house would be

the wedding party, so you don't need to worry about that. And as for hiring, any caterer will bring in their own people and bartenders. Everyone else should be easy to find and my mom can help."

"I'm still going to want to make it nice."

"I've been to the house a million times. It's already nice."

"We'll have to see about that." Taylor was already composing a mental to-do list. At the very least, many rooms would need fresh coats of paint, new linens and some sprucing up. "How many people are we talking?"

"We've capped it at one hundred for the ceremony. Thirty for the rehearsal dinner. We really don't want to make it a big deal," Chloe said.

Taylor's brain started gnawing on these bits of information. She loved a project. And she needed to keep her mind off the disastrous end to her two days with Roman. And since she loved Chloe, and could never say no to her, either, it was a no-brainer. "I'm going to need help from both of you."

"Did you just say yes?" Alex asked. "Chloe, I think Taylor said yes."

"And with so little convincing. How did that happen?" Chloe asked.

Taylor laughed quietly and took a sip of her wine. "It happened because I love you both and I need to stay busy."

"Isn't the whole hotel project going to keep you plenty busy? Add in this and I hope it won't end up being too much," Chloe said.

"Which is why I said that I'm going to need your help."

"Can we come up this week? The weather's supposed to be beautiful and I can work from there," Chloe said. "I'm itching to get started now."

"Ooh, yes," Alex interjected. "And since Chloe has hired me to do the flowers, I can say that technically I'm working, too. It will be like old times. Just the three of us and your amazing house."

Taylor was elated by the sound of all of this. A few days with her best friends? It not only sounded fun, it would definitely help her keep her brain on her two most urgent tasks—focusing on her summer estate project. And trying to forget about Roman Scott. "Sure thing. How soon can you guys get here?"

"Tomorrow morning? Can you do that, Alex?" Chloe asked.

"I'll start packing the minute we hang up. Does that work for you, Taylor?"

"Yep. I'll put some rosé in the fridge and make sure your bedrooms are ready. And while you're here, I can tell you what I found at Simone Astley's house."

"Oh, my God," Chloe said. "I completely forgot about that. Can you tell me anything now?"

"I have a bunch of photos to show you. I definitely think she was pregnant in one of them, but I'd love to hear your take on it. The big thing we discovered is that someone didn't want us there. There were sandbags piled against the only easy way in, and Roman and I both got threatening texts when we got back."

"Hold on a minute. Roman went with you? And you were threatened? Why don't I know about either of these things?" Chloe seemed genuinely aghast.

"Calm down, okay?" Taylor said. "Roman went with me because he didn't think I should go alone. And as for the threat, it was just that. A text. No big deal. Nothing has come of it."

"You take this stuff way too lightly," Alex said.

"It's not that I don't care. I just don't like to spend my energy worrying about things that I can't change."

"Hmm. Well, we'll talk about it when we get up there tomorrow," Chloe said. "Plus, I want to hear more about what happened with Roman."

"Me too," Alex added.

You're going to have to get at least one glass of wine in me before I spill the beans about Roman. "We'll see." Taylor said her goodbyes and hung up the phone. She might have to fend off her friends when it came to talking about Roman, but as for everything else they had to catch up on, she couldn't wait.

Eight

Whenever Roman flew anywhere, via plane or helicopter, he used that time to work. He read proposals, he researched new property opportunities or he simply wrote and returned emails. But on his flight back to Manhattan, he found himself leaning his head against the window, watching as the miles went by below and thinking a whole lot about everything that had happened with Taylor.

Granted, it wasn't a long flight from Connecticut into the city. A little more than a half hour. But it gave him plenty of time to think. Why was he feeling so torn about leaving her? Perhaps it was because they hadn't parted on great terms, sniping at each other about things like business philosophies or her calling him a genius. That was all on him. Taylor had thrown him off his game. Or maybe it was because of the threat from Little Black Book. He didn't need to live his life with a target on his back. Taylor and her friends could stir whatever pot they wanted to. He needed no part of that.

Logic said he needed distance. But despite having so many reasons to stay away from her, some long-forgotten part of him wanted to ask the pilot to turn around. He didn't do things like that. He didn't allow emotions and other people to disrupt his plans. He didn't change course. He was the man who marched forward into the future, leaving the past where it belonged. But he sure as hell thought about looking back for Taylor. And that had him worried.

What he was feeling was irrational. He and Taylor had only known each other for three days. That wasn't love. It wasn't even puppy love. It was infatuation, and at forty years old, if he was ever going to give himself another chance at love, it would be for something real and long-lasting. The only problem was he'd been so hurt and betrayed the first time he fell, that he'd convinced himself that a person only gets one real chance at love. He'd used his opportunity. It was gone.

He puttered around his apartment for an hour or so when he got home, unpacking his clothes, watering plants and throwing in a load of laundry—things he would have left to his housekeeper tomorrow if he hadn't returned early. He'd never thought of his place as anything less than pure luxury. He'd chosen every piece of furniture, artwork and finish. It was an oasis in the city, high above it all, built exactly for him. Now it felt like he'd washed up on a deserted island with no escape, destined to live there alone, forever. His solitary lifestyle hadn't bothered him in more than a decade. Once he got over Abby's death and everything that came to light after it, he embraced his single self. He liked not being tied to anyone else's needs or wants. He could do whatever he wanted, whenever he chose to do it. But somehow it was all feeling a bit sad and pathetic now.

Around 5:45, Roman met his driver down in the parking garage of his building. It was a short trip on a Sunday night to Derrick and Fiona's home. They traveled down 57th Street, then through Columbus Circle and then north along the western border of Central Park until they reached the Central Park West historic district, where Derrick and Fiona lived. Their building was built in the early 1900s, and they owned the top two floors, which included four bedrooms, a fully custom kitchen and a stunning terrace with dining area and a play structure for their daughter, Polly. They were less than a block's walk from the park, making it a wonderful place to raise a family.

"Thanks for coming," Derrick said when he answered the door.

"Of course." Roman gave his brother a hug.

"Fiona's finishing up with dinner. Polly's outside playing."

They strolled through the foyer and into the great room, a spacious living room and kitchen combined.

"Hello, Roman," Fiona said, stirring a large pot on the cooktop. "Dinner should be ready in fifteen."

Roman went up to his sister-in-law and kissed her cheek. "Smells amazing."

"Thanks. Nothing too fancy. Just some simple pasta sauce. In case your project with Derrick bankrupts us, I'll still be able to feed my family."

"Fiona. Do you really think I would let that happen?" Roman asked.

"Or me, for that matter?" Derrick added.

Fiona delivered a stern look to them both. "I just need you two to work it all out." She winced and rubbed her belly.

"Another contraction?" Derrick asked with a hard edge of worry in his voice. He was concerned for good reason. Polly had not only arrived a few weeks early, Fiona's labor had gone incredibly fast. She had the baby twenty minutes after they arrived at the hospital.

"They're just Braxton-Hicks. False labor. I'll know when the real thing happens. We have weeks."

"Can Derrick and I finish dinner for you?" Roman asked.

"No. Just go check on Polly."

Derrick kissed Fiona on the cheek. "Will do. She'll be mad if she finds out her uncle Roman is here and hasn't come to see her."

Roman followed his brother out to the terrace. It was a beautiful night, with a warm breeze. Sure enough, Polly was going down the slide of her cedar play structure, landing on a patch of artificial turf

Derrick and Fiona had installed. It was a pretty amazing setup for a kid in the city.

"Uncle Roman! Watch me!" Polly yelled, heading up the ladder.

"I'm watching. You're doing great," he called to her, then turned to Derrick. "Fiona doesn't seem superhappy about the project, but I guess it could be worse, right?"

He stuffed his hands into his pockets. "She's worried it'll take too long to get off the ground and we'll be stuck holding a loan forever. But I think it's just a lot to deal with now that she's close to her due date. It's only three weeks away."

"Totally understandable. I'll do my best over dinner to reassure her that it will be okay. There are lots of things we can do to bring in revenue before we open. And I'll reach out to the structural engineer personally to find out exactly what the holdup is." Roman didn't want to suggest it out loud, but sometimes a phone call from the person with their name on the check was all it took to make things happen quicker.

"Perfect. Thank you. You know I never work with existing structures. I'm always either starting new or tearing down the old. It's a whole new world working on a building that's been around for so long."

"It's part of what's so rewarding about it. Giving a beautiful building a new life. You'll get the hang of it. Then you'll have another weapon in your arsenal if you ever decide to pivot to something new."

"Yeah. Maybe." Derrick shrugged. "I'm sorry I

brought you back from Connecticut early. How was it giving advice to Taylor Klein?"

Roman immediately felt heat rushing to his cheeks. "It was interesting. That's for sure."

Derrick made eye contact, silently probing for more details. "What is that tone in your voice?"

"Nothing," he said, quickly noticing how defensive he sounded. "She has a great project on her hands. She's turning her family's summer estate into a boutique hotel. The property is gorgeous and she has room to grow. She could have quite a gold mine there. That's what we talked about."

"Interesting. It's exactly what you do. Turning something old into something new. Is she trying to follow in your footsteps?"

"It's a similar thing. And she mentioned being inspired by my properties. But I encouraged her to make it her own. We talked a lot about that."

Derrick arched an eyebrow at Roman, seeming unconvinced. "I don't mind saying that she's a beautiful woman. And she's single. Did anything happen that didn't involve talking?"

Roman cleared his throat, unsure how to put this. Ultimately, he decided that honesty was the best course, even when he knew his brother was going to probe for more. "A few things."

"A few?" Derrick playfully hit Roman's shoulder. "This is seriously the best news I have ever heard."

"You don't even know what happened."

"Do you want to tell me?"

"No. I do not."

"Fair enough. I won't pry. It just makes me happy." He glanced back at the house. "It will make Fiona giddy. We have to tell her. It might improve her mood."

"Don't bring it up, okay? Especially not at dinner."

"Why not?"

"Because what happened is over and I don't think there's going to be anything else beyond that. I mean, in the future." Roman knew he was rambling. It was painfully obvious, at least to him, that he was so far out of his depth in talking about this. That worried him. Taylor had really worked her way into his psyche. She'd gotten to him. Big-time.

"Did you torch the whole thing?" Derrick asked.

"A little? Maybe? I mean, we got into an argument or a heated discussion about her property. She was asking for my advice, but what she really wanted was for me to tell her exactly what to do. And I just don't believe in that. If she's going to own the project, she needs to own it. It should be her vision. Her baby."

Derrick stared at Roman, silent, only blinking for a good thirty seconds after he'd finished talking. "You do realize that not everyone is you, right?"

"What's that supposed to mean?"

"Your skill set is not something everyone possesses. If they did, there would be a million Roman Scotts wandering the earth, and luckily for us all, there's only one."

"Look, I didn't say those things lightly. Taylor is clearly brilliant. And I know she's creative. This whole idea comes from a place of inventiveness. And she has so much enthusiasm for the project, that it's infectious. I know that she can come up with something if she just learns to trust herself. She'll be so proud of it when she's done if she takes that route."

"Wow."

"What?"

"You are completely smitten with her. And you blew it up? I knew you were capable of personal self-sabotage, but I didn't realize it was this bad. I guess I figured that at this point, you would have enough sense to keep things in a good place if you met a woman you were seriously interested in."

"I'm not self-sabotaging. This is just the way things played out." Of course, there was one additional factor Derrick didn't know about—that threat from Little Black Book. That was part of the reason he'd left so abruptly. It freaked him out to no end. "I'm not going to lie to her or tell her something I don't believe in."

Derrick drew in a deep breath and blew it out through his nose, the flare of his nostrils demonstrating exactly how frustrated he was with Roman. "How did you leave it?"

"I wished her good luck and I left. She has my number. She knows how to reach me if she needs help."

"You need to call her and apologize."

"You don't know that. You weren't there." Although Roman could admit to himself that he did probably need to smooth things over with Taylor. He'd at least sleep better knowing that she didn't hate him. He'd like to be able to talk to her if they ever ran into each other again. Hell, he'd like to be able to talk to her again, period.

"I know women. Apologize. You will never go wrong with telling a woman that you're sorry."

"Okay."

"I'm serious."

"Fine."

"And if the look in your eyes is any indication of how you feel about her, you need to find a way to see her again. As soon as humanly possible."

"I'm busy. My schedule is a nightmare."

"Hey, guys," Fiona said from the doorway into the kitchen. "Dinner's on. Can you get Polly and help her wash her hands?"

"Yeah, hon. I've got it," Derrick said. As soon as Fiona ducked back inside, he gave Roman a final brotherly glare. "If you truly like her, you'll find a way to be less busy. And I'm thinking that you really like her."

Roman sighed as he watched Derrick walk over to the play structure and scoop up Polly. He knew his brother was right. He was always right. He'd been right about everything with Abby. And he was right about everything now. It was just that Roman wasn't sure he was ready to make that leap. If he gave even a fraction of his heart to Taylor and it didn't work out, could he count on his brother to help him pick up the pieces one more time? Derrick had a new baby on the way, an occasionally unhappy wife and a young daughter. He had enough on his plate. Roman needed to sink or swim on his own. For now, it felt safest to keep paddling and spend less time thinking about Taylor Klein.

Having her girlfriends at the estate was the best thing in the world for Taylor. By the end of their first day together, she felt much more like her old self, but in the best possible way. She'd been able to focus on the task at hand—the estate and Chloe's wedding. She'd spent time looking forward, exactly what she needed.

"Do you feel like we've got a good start on everything for the wedding?" Taylor asked. The three were sitting out by the pool, enjoying a bottle of rosé, along with some cheese and crackers.

Chloe was poring over the notebook she'd brought along. "Yes. I mean, we'll have a million details to work out, and I'm sure I'll have a ton of questions after I talk to my mom. But for right now, I think we've made a good start."

Taylor already had a long list of things she needed to do to the house, but in discussing these things with Chloe and Alex, she'd been able to get her creative juices flowing, and those ideas were spilling into ideas for the hotel. She'd come up with what she thought would be a brilliant idea for the massive formal dining room. She could see it transformed into an intimate restaurant with cozy circular booths, dark lighting and a killer bar in the corner. She had an entire page of notes about her design ideas for it, including the color scheme, fabrics and general layout. That was a project for after the wedding, but it gave her something to look forward to. It excited her to know that she was capable of coming up with a vision. Just like Roman had stubbornly insisted she do.

"I love the idea of Parker and I exchanging vows out in the clearing on the other side of the woods, overlooking the sound. It's so beautiful and private up there," Chloe said.

"Oh, good. I'm glad you like that." It had come to Taylor when they were walking the grounds and she remembered that she'd shown the overlook to Roman. He'd said it was special, and she had to agree. Of course, thinking about him only brought up her mixed emotions about their time together. She could admit to herself that the instant she started getting ideas about the hotel, the first person she'd wanted to share them with was Roman. But he likely thought she was a fool, and he was back in the city, living the fabulous life of Roman Scott. Maybe if she let things sit for a few weeks, she might muster the nerve to call him and give him an update. If she handled things well, they might be able to manage a friendship. Even if that was the only thing she ever got from him, she would like that very much.

"So, you still haven't told us about Roman," Alex said, refilling her glass then topping off both Chloe's and Taylor's.

"I already told you most of this, Alex. He was helpful, but only to a point. I think he really wanted to push me to come up with a plan for the hotel all on my own. Without any input from him."

"Which I said was stupid," Alex said.

"But is it?" Chloe sat back in her chair and crossed her legs. "I mean, the man has come up with all sorts of hotel ideas on his own. I'm guessing that either he didn't have more to share, or he wanted you to approach it the same way he did. Maybe his success isn't so much about his ideas, but the way he tackles his projects."

"Could be," Taylor said. "It mostly made me feel like I didn't know what I was doing, and I've already spent most of my life feeling that way, so it was not superfun." *Some parts were fun. Incredibly fun.*

"What was he like?" Alex asked.

Taylor took another sip of her wine, realizing that she was already feeling a bit tipsy, and that was when she had a tendency to overshare. "He's amazing. Supersmart. Witty. Surprisingly fun. Ridiculously handsome. He's basically everything a woman could ever want in a man."

"And?" Chloe asked. "Did you get to partake of this man who is everything a woman could ever want?"

Taylor didn't know what to say. She still wasn't sure she wanted to share this.

Alex shot Taylor a penetrating gaze. "Tell us, Taylor. You know you want to."

She hesitated a few more moments, but knew that her friends were going to drag this out of her eventually. "Yes. A few times."

Alex squealed. "Tell us everything."

"No way," Taylor replied.

"Will you at least tell us if it was good?" Chloe asked with an inquisitive quirk of her eyebrow.

"Completely and totally amazing." She could have added more superlatives to her review of Roman's seductive ways, but sometimes the simplest words were the best.

"But? I sense a but," Chloe said.

"Of course you do. You sense a but because there is one. As in, *but* I promised myself I would stay away from men."

"I don't want to keep labeling things as stupid, but in this case, I'll make an exception," Alex said. "That's stupid." She reached out and grasped Taylor's forearm. "No offense."

"Maybe it is. It's the only thing that makes sense to me."

"But you had sex with a superhot guy," Alex insisted. "That's not nothing."

"Sex is great, but it's not enough," Taylor said. "I'm tired of having my heart broken. I'm tired of feeling like I'm not good enough. And I'm just not capable of divorcing the two things from each other. To me, sex leads to feelings. It happens every time."

"Nobody likes feeling like they aren't good enough. But maybe it's just that you haven't met the right person. And maybe all of that bad luck you've had is only because the right person is going to be so extra amazing that you won't even believe it." Alex smiled wide when she was done sharing her little theory.

"So says the endless optimist," Chloe said.

"Hey. I might be right," Alex shot back.

"You might. Or you might not," Taylor said. "But the thing about Roman is that I can't imagine him thinking about me. I'm sure he hasn't given me a second thought since he left." She didn't want it to sound as though she was pitying herself. She wasn't. These were truths that she believed deep in her soul. And she'd learned that being honest with herself was always the best course. It kept her grounded. It made things real.

"It's his loss if that's the case," Alex said. "But I also think you should stay open to the possibilities."

"Can we please talk about something else?" Taylor asked, reaching for a cracker and some brie.

"I can't stop thinking about those Simone Astley photos," Alex said. She and Chloe had asked to talk about Simone pretty much as soon as they'd walked through the front door. "She's definitely pregnant. And I have to think that's the reason her mother pulled her out of Baldwell and didn't put her in a different school."

"That's a pretty safe assumption," Chloe said. "From everything my grandmother said about her mom, she was very judgmental. Concerned with appearances."

"Maybe the next step is to ask Parker's investigator to look into birth records. If she had a baby, they had to go somewhere, right?" Taylor couldn't stop thinking about what she and Roman had discovered in the basement, in the servants' quarters. "And what do you guys think about the child's bedroom we found?"

"That's what has me stumped," Chloe said. "If Simone had a baby, they wouldn't have lived in the basement. Plus, Simone was living in that house the whole time and from everything you said, the room was for a young child. Her kid would have to be in their early to midfifties by now. If they're still alive."

"Or ever existed," Taylor said.

"So it was probably a member of the staff who had a child," Alex added.

"That makes more sense." Taylor sat back in her chair and finished her glass of wine, looking out at the grounds. The whole thing was intriguing, even if it was frustrating to still not have a clear picture of what had happened and how that led to the creation of Little Black Book. Then again, maybe the mystery was the point. Little Black Book did not want anyone to know what had happened.

The three opened another bottle of wine and talked until well past sunset. Alex, always a champion sleeper, was the first to yawn. "I know I'm lame, but I'm so tired," she said.

"Yeah. I need to catch up on email. I did zero work today and I'm sure my inbox is a disaster." Chloe got up from her chair.

"Sounds like a plan. I want to work on my to-do list for the wedding. And I also need to write up some more of my ideas for the house," Taylor said. "And the first contractor is coming by tomorrow."

"I need to put you in touch with Ryder, too," Alex said.

"Indeed you do."

They collected the dishes and empty wine bottles, carried everything into the kitchen, then headed upstairs.

"Is there anything either of you need?" Taylor asked.

"Just a good night's sleep," Alex answered.

"Perfect. I'll see you both in the morning."

"Good night, Taylor," Chloe said. "And thank you for everything." She closed her bedroom door.

Taylor ducked inside her own room and flopped down on her bed, tired but exhilarated. She caught herself pondering not washing her face and simply going to bed in her clothes. It was a very bad idea, but so tempting. Just as she'd decided she had to get up, her phone beeped with a text. When she saw that it was from Roman, her heart fluttered. It skipped an actual beat. Checking on you. Everything okay?

She smiled at her phone, imagining his voice. His face. His lips when he spoke. I'm good. You?

Better now that I know you're good. Can we talk?

She read the question several times and tapped the side of her phone with her finger. Was this a good idea? Probably not. Did she want to talk to him? Absolutely. Of course. Her phone was ringing mere seconds later. "Hey, there," she answered. "How are you? What are you up to?"

"I just got home from the office. It was a long day, but thank you for asking."

Taylor glanced at her alarm clock on the bedside

table. It was a little after ten. "That's way too long a day. You must be exhausted."

"I am. I was. But I have a little more energy now that I can talk to you." He cleared his throat. "Are you sure you're okay? Nothing weird with Little Black Book? I felt strange leaving you there by yourself."

"Nothing weird from Little Black Book. And I'm actually not by myself. My friends Alex and Chloe came up for a few days. Chloe has decided she wants to have her wedding here over Labor Day weekend."

"Does that mean you're putting the hotel plans on hold?"

"Not really. Touring the house with my friends and talking about the wedding really helped me get a bunch of ideas about what I want to do. So I figure I can spend the next two months planning, then hopefully kick the real renovations into gear for the fall."

"So, you feel good about it?"

She had an inkling of what he was getting at. "Yes. I do. You were right. I needed to take full ownership of the project. I definitely feel better about it now. I'm more excited about it. Probably more than I would have been if you'd spoon-fed it to me."

"Good. I'm glad. That makes me really happy to hear. I think the wedding is a wonderful idea. It could give you a taste of what it takes to run a hotel. Of course, I say that but I never actually do the running. I do the top-level work then let someone else take over."

"Well, it's not going to be like that for me. I need to be much more hands-on."

"I suppose I could stand to do some more hands-on work."

Taylor couldn't escape the double meaning in those words, the way his voice dipped lower and got supersexy.

"Taylor, I need to tell you something."

"Okay…"

"I know this is going to sound absurd and probably wildly inappropriate…"

If he'd been wanting to pique her interest, he absolutely had. "Just say what you want to say, Roman. You will never go wrong with me and complete honesty."

"I miss you."

The air around her seemed to stop moving. Had the earth stopped spinning as well? She might have dated dozens and dozens of men, but not a single one had ever said that to her. It was such a sweet and simple statement—three little words that were not *I love you* but still meant a lot. And yet, no guy had allowed them to pass his lips. "You do?"

"I won't blame you if you want to hang up on me. I realize we didn't leave things on the best terms. And I understand how sappy that sounds. God, I'm glad we're on the phone so I don't have to see your face right now. Even though I love looking at your face."

Her mind was whirring at top speed, wondering what this meant, then questioning whether that meant she was reading too much into it. "Shut up, Roman. Please. Just stop talking."

"Okay."

She couldn't remember ever taking in a deeper breath, but she needed the strength to take the leap. Some women might not care about *I miss you*, but she did. It implied something deeper than lust, something more than *you're okay*. It suggested the thing she'd always been looking for but that had proved so elusive—real and honest feelings. "I miss you, too, Roman. I've missed you since the minute you left."

"Even with your friends there? I'm sure you were busy."

"They're a nice distraction, for sure. And I'm excited about everything I need to work on, but I still miss you." She scooted down farther in her bed and gnawed on her fingernail. "I still thought about you when I went to bed last night."

"Oh, really?"

"Yes, really."

"What did you think about?"

She smiled at the seductive tone in his voice. It made her skin come alive with electricity. "I thought about kissing you. I thought about how hot you look in those pajama pants."

He unleashed a breathy laugh. "They *are* sexy."

You're sexy. "I thought about taking off your clothes and touching you."

He groaned quietly into the phone. "If we're going to make confessions, I've been thinking about you nonstop, Taylor. You won't leave my brain. No matter how hard I try."

"Have you been trying? To get me out of your mind?"

"Not really."

This made her so ridiculously happy that it felt like her heart might grow wings and fly out of her body. "So where does that leave us?"

"I want to see you. I need to see you. Can you come to the city?"

However tempting the invitation, Taylor had an awful lot of experience bending over backward to suit a man's wants and desires, and she had much to prove to herself in this situation. Yes, he'd said he missed her. That was a start. But was he willing to go out of his way for her? "I would love to see you, but I can't leave the estate. Now that I'm planning a wedding, it's just so busy. I have all sorts of contractor meetings lined up."

"Unfortunately, my schedule is just as hectic."

Her stomach sank. She'd pushed for too much. "Of course."

"But I'm also the boss. And certain perks come with that. Like leaving whenever the hell I want to."

She grinned so wide it made it hard to see. "You're really selling me on the idea of being my own boss."

"I might only be able to come for a night, but I will make it happen. When are your friends leaving?"

"Friday morning."

"I can be there by lunchtime."

"Seriously?"

"I've never been more serious about anything in all my life."

Nine

Roman had never been so eager for the helicopter to land. All he could think about was what was waiting for him once he was on the ground—Taylor. It had been three days of biding his time, all of which had been sheer torture. Hours ticked by at a snail's pace. And now, as he hovered above her family's estate, then dipped lower, he spotted her and his heart crept up into his throat. She was standing by the pool in a blue sundress, holding her hand to her forehead to shield her eyes from the setting sun. He was instantly struck by memories of the short time they'd spent together—her smell, her smile, her taste. And he knew then that this had been the best decision. He'd had every reason to feel some reservation about this, but coming to see her had been the right choice.

He felt like a man marching back from battle victorious as he strode across the grass and climbed the gentle slope up to the back patio and the pool, Taylor grinning at him all the way. He'd found a way to get back here. To get back to her. And she seemed as happy to see him as he was to see her. "Hello, you," he said, dropping his bag to the flagstone and taking her hand.

"Hello, yourself." She drifted in to him, and closed her eyes partway, but she didn't kiss him. He was left to his own devices.

And he took the opportunity with both hands, pulling her into his arms, clutching the back of her head with one hand and bestowing the hottest I-want-you kiss he could muster on her luscious lips. She responded in kind, angling her head to the side and slipping her tongue into his mouth. It was everything he'd been thinking about for the last few days. And more.

"Are you hungry? I was planning on making you dinner. Roast chicken and a salad?"

Was she kidding with dinner? Roman was well acquainted with his needs at that moment and they weren't for that kind of sustenance. He cupped Taylor's shoulders, his fingers caressing her arms, silky and bare in the sleeveless dress. Normally patient, cool and collected, Roman had been anything but that as he'd waited to see her today. Now that they were together, alone, he'd reached the point of no return. "I'm not really hungry. But let's go inside."

"Okay."

He scooped up his bag and followed her in through the mudroom.

Taylor stopped in the kitchen. "Something to drink?"

He didn't want that, either. He dropped his bag on the floor and pulled her into another embrace, kissing her neck while he reached for the zipper on her dress, noting each click the pull made as he tugged it lower. Those clicks meant she was one step closer to being his, but hearing them wasn't enough right now. He wanted to see every inch of her. He turned her around, which elicited a sweet sigh of approval from Taylor.

He drew the zipper down until it stopped, teasing the dress open, placing kisses along the channel of her spine as he went.

"I'm not really hungry anyway." She softened beneath his touch as everything in his body became more rigid and overheated.

"I am, but not for food."

She curved her back and pressed her luscious bottom against his crotch and he groaned with determination. Everything below his waist had felt heavy since he'd laid eyes on her. He throbbed for Taylor, and she was only making his need more unrelenting.

He countered her pressure, flattening himself against her, harder, pulling the straps from her shoulders and away from her body. He nudged her hair aside with his nose, returning to the heaven of her neck, peppering it with wet, open-mouthed kisses as the dress fell to the floor.

He reached around and placed his hand flat against her belly, pressing her body against his. She craned her neck back to kiss him, reaching up and cupping the back of his head with her hand. Her lips were impossibly soft, a respite from hard reality. He wanted to get lost in them, have them get lost on him. He slipped his hand between her back and his chest, needing to stay in as much close contact with her as possible, and unhooked her bra. She dropped her hand from his neck, shrugging the straps until they slid slowly down her arms and met the same fate as her dress.

Being this much closer to the main attraction only made him that much more restless to reach it. She was down to black satin panties and that was it. As much as he wanted her naked in his arms, he wanted to experience every sensory pleasure imaginable. So he reached down and teased her center with his fingers, through the soft fabric. "Roman," she gasped from that most insignificant touch.

"Yes?" he asked, delivering the question straight into her ear.

"Everything you're doing to me feels so good."

"I had several days to think about this. To fantasize about everything I wanted to do to you." He loved having her at his mercy, his for the taking. He took both of her hands and lifted her arms high up over her head, urging her to reach for the back of his neck. The fingers of his right hand smoothed over her belly in gentle, teasing strokes. Her skin was so delicate and her breathing so pronounced, there were times when a whisper-thin sliver of space was left between their skin and a current still traveled between them. He kissed her neck softly, gently nibbled on her ear, all while a low hum came from Taylor's lips and the warm ambient light from the windows cast the room in a beautiful glow.

He swept his hand up between her breasts, using only the pads of his fingers, propagating goose bumps as he went. He then reversed course and dragged the back of his hand down to her belly button, building tension between them when he didn't think he could take it much longer. "You want me to touch your breasts, don't you?" he huffed into her ear. He ached to have them in his hands, but he also longed to hear her say the words. He'd noticed before the way she liked it so much when he touched her there, when he licked her nipples.

"I do, Roman. I do."

"I'm only here to make you happy." He heard her anxious breathing, sensed her anticipation of his caress. Unable to leave her waiting, he cupped the underside of her smooth breast, smiling when she trembled beneath his touch. He grazed her tight nipple with his thumb.

She leaned back into him, restlessly grinding against his crotch, conjuring a deep groan from his throat. She whipped around and faced him, tearing into his lips like a woman whose desires could never be quenched. Of course, he sure as hell was going to try. Her fingers fumbled with the buttons of his shirt as he had the presence of mind to unbuckle his belt and rid himself of his trousers and boxer briefs.

He reached down and squeezed her velvety ass, trailing his hand down the back of one thigh and lifting it until her leg was hitched over his hips. Their bodies were almost at war, however good it felt, and he was starting to feel like he might not make it to the final battle as she was still in her panties. His raging erection rubbed over the smooth silk, making it impossible to think straight.

Taylor was struggling to balance on one leg, so he let go, and turned to his bag, opening it frantically and pulling out a condom from his toiletry kit. Then he scooped her into his arms and carried her into the study. As soon as they crossed the threshold and he set her down, she walked backward, curling her finger in invitation. "Come here, you."

Even in the softer light of this room, he could see her happy grin and it made him elated. "What do you have for me?"

Taylor stopped when the back of her calves met the large circular ottoman in the center of the room. "Maybe this." She shimmied her panties past her hips and kicked them aside, then reclined on the soft surface, resting on her elbows, a true feast for the senses.

He was consumed by a whole new level of need, and ripped open the condom packet and quickly rolled it on. She leaned farther back and scooted her bottom to the very edge of the ottoman as he dropped to his knees between her legs. He grabbed one of her ankles and placed it on his shoulder, then teased apart her folds, driving two fingers inside. She was beyond ready—warm and inviting. "You're so wet," he muttered, clearing the gravel from his voice.

Her head dropped back as he thrust and twisted his fingers. She looked back at him when he hit the sweet spot—that sensitive bundle of nerves that made a woman squirm. "I want you, Roman."

That was like the starting pistol and his erection somehow got even harder, like it wanted to vie with his hand for the privilege of being inside her. He poised himself at her entrance and drove inside. Again her head dropped back, and a gasping moan left her lips. "You feel so good," she said.

Good didn't begin to describe how perfect she felt. She had him in her grip, her body holding on to him tight. This was the only place he wanted to be, not only because of his physical needs. He wanted to be with no other human on the earth at that moment. He wanted no one else to exist. He wanted it to be the two of them, together, unbothered by the rest of the world.

He clutched one hip with his hand while trailing the other along the outside of her thigh, gripping her ankle, turning his head and kissing her ankle softly. He thrust with careful purpose, taking long strokes, rounding his hips at the end, which he'd now learned made her really happy.

She sat up, propping herself up on her elbows again, countering the force of his hips with her own. Her eyes were dark and intense. Her lips went slack as her breaths became ragged. She looked directly at him, unafraid. He felt in that moment like he knew her on a much deeper level. This was Taylor, the woman he couldn't get out of his mind.

He drove harder, his thighs hitting the ottoman when he met her. His knees were screaming for relief, and he shifted one of his legs until his foot was on the floor, giving himself far more leverage. He was about to burst from the tension that had built inside him. He closed his eyes—the visual of Taylor was far too enticing, but that made the sensation of her wrapped around him that much more heightened. This was the fantasy he'd been consumed by for the last few days, and he had it. For real.

As if the universe understood just how much effort he was putting into not letting go, Taylor sucked in a sharp breath, her chin dropped to her chest and she quaked, her thighs trembling. He gave way, in a torrent of fierce waves of pleasure. No words were uttered. No words were possible as the force coursed through him, shuddering his entire body as they both tried to reclaim their breath.

He leaned down and pulled her into his arms, stroking the smooth skin of her back with one hand while the other tangled in her silky hair. They fell into a kiss that was deep and intense, one that spoke of a familiarity far beyond the days on the calendar. He and Taylor had connected on a molecular level. There was something here, and for the first time in forever, he wasn't afraid by the notion of finding out what it was.

* * *

Hours after Roman's arrival, Taylor was regularly reminding herself to slow down, but it wasn't easy. She was struggling to understand how she'd gone through even a minute of her life without him. That scene in the kitchen? So hot. The study? Even hotter. And then they'd ended up in her bathroom, showering, and making each other happy in an entirely different way. She'd had good sex, but this was a whole new level. This was an awakening. It didn't mean that her vow to stay away from men was gone. She simply knew now that the promise should have been to stay away from every guy who wasn't Roman. *Hindsight,* she told herself, *was twenty-twenty.*

She did manage to make him dinner and they ate at the kitchen island, drinking wine and kissing between bites. It wasn't so much about satisfying an urge to eat so much as it felt like fuel for later. But it occurred to her that as electric as their physical connection was, she wanted to know more about Roman, more than the things she'd learned in an internet search or the few little breadcrumbs he'd left for her along the way.

"Roman, can I ask you a question?" They'd just finished cleaning up the kitchen and Taylor was about to start the dishwasher.

"I think you just did." He leaned against the kitchen counter, wearing a different pair of pajama pants than the ones he'd worn during his first visit. It was an impressive wardrobe of loungewear—he looked stunning in all of it.

"I'm serious." She wiped her hands with the dish towel. "I have a feeling you don't want to talk about it, but I do want to know about your wife. Only because I want to know more about you. And in my experience, you learn the most about a person when you find out the things that have hurt them."

He nodded and a faint smile crossed his lips. "You are a very intuitive person, Taylor. That's why I was so eager for you to follow your gut when it came to this house."

She reached out and tugged at his hip. "And there's plenty of time to talk about that later. But I want to know what happened. Or I at least want to know that you don't want to tell me. Because that will say a lot about where I stand with you."

He knocked his head to one side. "Well, that's one way to put it."

She shrugged. "I'm just saying this feels like way more than a hookup."

"It is."

"Then let's find out more about each other."

He drew in a deep breath through his nose. "Let's grab a bottle of wine and find a comfortable spot to sit."

"Good idea." Taylor opened a bottle of zinfandel, and they went into the study. She flicked on the fireplace for some ambience and they cozied up on the couch together.

"It'll be a lot easier for me to share what happened to me if you'll tell me at least a little about all of these men who were idiotic enough to break your heart," Roman said as he got settled.

She sensed that whatever he had to share would be far more profound than any story she might tell, but she also wanted this to be a free exchange. She wanted to be open with him. "There's a long list of names. Too long to mention. The ones that hurt the most were Ian, Malik and Bradley. Bradley was in college. He was sleeping with my roommate. I broke up with them both, but really I was the one who got dumped. It's not like I chose for that to happen. I met Malik when I was working as an events planner. His company hired us and I fell for him hard. That lasted several months, but then I found out that he was seeing his ex on the side. Ian was a little less than a year ago. He and I met at a bar. Honestly, he was a goofball, but I have a habit of falling for charming men. He had a girlfriend in LA. Or rather he now has a fiancée in LA. They're getting married."

"Wow." He took a sip of his wine.

"There's more. A whole lot more. But most aren't worth mentioning."

"If they hurt you, they're worth mentioning."

"You know, I don't think it's the long string of guys that bothers me. It's the message I kept getting over and over, which is that I, for whatever reason, wasn't enough."

He nodded, seeming to take it all in. Meanwhile, the fire cast his face in an unbelievable glow. "And it sounds like you've felt that same way with your career choices. So that can't be helping. It seems to me like it's all holding you back."

She'd never heard anyone put it into such plain terms. It felt so good to know that he understood why she felt the way she did. "Exactly. And now you hopefully see why I was so reluctant to boldly follow my gut, especially around you, when I was already intimidated. It wasn't an easy thing."

"I get that now. Completely."

"But being with my girlfriends over the last few days really helped. I guess I could let down my guard with them, and that's what got the creative juices going."

A clever smirk crossed his lips. "It seems like you're getting better at letting down your guard with me."

She smiled and leaned over to kiss him. "I might be going right to the head of the class."

"You're getting straight As and doing all of your extra credit from where I'm sitting," he said.

She laughed, then sat back and delivered him an inquisitive glance. She'd shared. Now she wanted him to do the same. "So? You ready to tell me about your wife?"

"Her name was Abby Reynolds," he started, taking another sip of his wine, only it was a much longer drink this time. "We met when I was twenty-four, a couple of years out of college, and getting the first hotel property going in Boston. She worked at the restaurant next door, and I was in there all the time during construction." He raked a hand through his hair, his eyes stormy and a bit overwhelmed, his hesitancy over talking about this bubbling to the surface. "She pulled me in from the very beginning. She was smart and funny. And she was all alone. No family. No real friends. She'd only been in Boston for a while. She didn't come from money, had worked hard her whole life and been on her own since she was a teenager. It seemed like she was the salt of the earth and she very quickly became my everything."

Taylor shifted in her seat, fighting back this odd sense of jealousy. Abby was gone, but she'd had Roman's heart, and that was an enviable position. "She sounds wonderful."

"She *seemed* wonderful. That's the difference." He reached for the wine bottle and poured himself another glass, then went ahead and topped off Taylor's. "So yes. We fell in love. She moved in with me. She said that she'd really wanted to start a restaurant, so I went to my parents and got her a chunk of money to lease a space and buy equipment. I helped her pick it out. We were making all kinds of plans. And then one day I come home and she tells me that she's pregnant."

"Oh, wow." That was a turn in the tale Taylor had not anticipated. "Plot twist."

"To say the least. So, I went to my parents and told them what was going on and my mom gave me my great-grandmother's wedding ring to propose. Abby said yes, but she wanted a very small ceremony. And she did not want to get married in Massachusetts. I thought it was a little strange at the time, but I figured she knew what she wanted, and she had no family to worry about, so I let her decide everything. We got married up in Maine in a tiny chapel with just my parents, my brother and Fiona there."

Taylor knew that the end of the story was coming soon and she braced for it.

"We postponed the honeymoon because the Boston hotel was close to opening. Two weeks later, I was on-site at the hotel, and state troopers show up to tell me that Abby had been in a car accident. She went off a bridge. She was dead."

Taylor reached for Roman, purely out of instinct. "Oh, my God. It was so sudden. That had to have been so hard."

"I was in shock. Completely numb. But the hours and days after that was when I got the real shock. That's when I found out the truth about her."

"Which was?"

"She wasn't who she said she was. Her name wasn't Abby. It was Caroline Kupchek. And she'd been married four other times. She was still married to one guy. She was a con artist. She'd lied to me about everything. I was a mark and she took me for a ride."

Taylor clasped her hand over her mouth and she knew her eyes were impossibly wide, but she could not believe this story. It was unreal. "Roman. No. Seriously?"

He nodded. "Seriously."

"Was she really pregnant?"

"I don't know. We'll never know." He sighed.

"I'm so sorry. No wonder you don't want to talk about it."

"Well, unfortunately, that wasn't the half of it. She'd emptied one of my bank accounts. She took the money my parents gave her for the restaurant. And she'd actually taken all of her stuff out of our apartment. So she was leaving that day she died."

"And your grandmother's ring?"

"Don't know what happened to that, either. She wasn't wearing it when she died and they didn't find it in the car. She most likely pawned it, but we don't know where it went."

"So she just left behind this complete path of destruction."

"She did. My parents were horrified. And I sort of thought they might feel sorry for me, but they were really embarrassed. And they were worried about what it might mean if this all got out in the press. It could have ruined my dad's career. He was pondering a run in politics at the time. It would have dragged my family name through the mud, and of course, it could have made it really hard to launch my business if all people were talking about was that I had been tricked by this woman."

"And that's why you scrubbed your past."

He nodded. "Yes. That's why. As it turned out, the only thing she didn't lie to me about was having no family. Other than the other husband, of course. And she didn't have any children, thank goodness. Our marriage was very quietly annulled. And then my brother and I hired a private cyber security firm and they very meticulously got rid of my history with her."

This was all starting to come together, and it broke her heart. "Which is why it's like the Boston hotel magically appeared and then your career went on from there."

"Right. Except, a reporter figured it out a week after the grand opening in Boston. And he was relentless. Luckily, he wasn't able to find much, but he followed me around for weeks and weeks. Spying on me. Having photographers tail me. Calling and needling me for information. That's why I can't stand the press. It just put such a bad taste in my mouth. I was trying so hard to turn my life around and get a fresh start and he was determined to make a name for himself with a few juicy headlines. I eventually just left town and moved on to opening my second hotel, crossing my fingers that he'd stop chasing the story. And he did, obviously, since nothing ever came of it. After that, I just put my head down and worked hard and tried very very hard to forget about Abby."

Taylor set her wineglass on the table and pulled Roman into a hug, holding on to him tight. "I'm so sorry that happened. I can't even imagine what that would have been like."

He returned the embrace, and she fit perfectly in his arms. "You know, I almost think that keeping the secret is part of what has made it worse. Nobody knows other than my family. Not even my closest work associates. Definitely no one I've been romantically involved with." He loosened his grip on her, looking her right in the eye.

"I understand. It's been really hard for me to trust anyone."

"Of course."

"And obviously it's been hard for you, too." She smiled softly, wondering what she'd done to be so lucky to not only meet Roman, but for their relationship to turn into this.

"It has. But I feel good about trusting you. I feel like it was the right decision to listen to my gut." His hand went to her jaw, his thumb tracing the end of her chin. "It's very important." He leaned in and delivered a soul-gripping kiss, one that left her lips buzzing with excitement. "Just like I think it's important for us to go upstairs to your room."

"To get some sleep?"

He shook his head and chuckled to himself. "Eventually. Maybe."

He got up from the couch and reached for her hand. Taylor coiled her fingers around his and they started out of the room. Every step forward with Roman felt so much more consequential now. He'd been through so much and yet he chose to spend time with her. He'd called her and said that he missed her. He came back to her. And maybe that was what had been missing for Taylor before. Those other guys simply hadn't meant much. Not like Roman Scott.

Ten

Roman didn't stay only one night. He stayed for three. And it was the most magical stretch of time that Taylor could remember. She didn't want to go so far as to think that this was turning into love, but it was definitely *something*. It had been worth it to break her promise to herself. Roman was the most amazing man she'd ever met—smart, funny and kind. Sexy, strong and yet unafraid to be human with her.

When they weren't in bed, which was often, they were walking the property, talking about Taylor's plans. Roman seemed impressed by everything she'd come up with since the first time he'd been there.

The subject came up on that Monday morning, when they were sneaking in a cup of coffee and a croissant before he had to head back to the city. He had plans to meet his brother later that morning so they could discuss their project. "The hotel is going to be so beautiful when you're done. I can't wait to see it all come together."

"Thanks. I'm excited, too. Of course, I have a lot to do before the wedding, too."

"I think it's a good thing. You'll get your feet wet with the contractors. You'll be able to figure out who you like working with, but at a time when it's not quite so consequential. Then you can move forward with the people you trust."

Taylor couldn't ignore how much of what he was saying applied to their personal entanglements. She wanted to move forward with Roman. She trusted him. How had that happened in such a short period of time? It boggled the mind and yet it still seemed to make sense. "I can't tell you how much I appreciate you walking me through all of this. The support is such a huge help."

"I just want you to know that there will be times when you're pulling out your hair. And you'll feel like you can't do it, or you'll never get it done. It will get overwhelming. But I will be here for you every step of the way. I've already made every mistake a hotelier could make. Someone should be able to learn from everything I've messed up. So, yeah, anything you need, just let me know."

Taylor was a little taken aback by the offer, even though Roman had shown her time and time again that he was a very generous man, this was still an extraordinary pledge of help. She felt nothing less than extremely fortunate to have him in her life. "Thank you so much. I really appreciate that. I will definitely call you whenever I need advice. And of course, I'm hoping that you'll come to visit a fair amount."

He leaned in closer and gave her a kiss. "Actually, I'm about to have an extra excuse to come to Connecticut. Remember when I told you that I attended Sedgefield Academy?"

"I do."

"I give money every year as an alum, but I'm about to move forward with a bigger partnership with them. I'm paying for and coordinating the construction of a new building for the history and English departments. I just got confirmation from the school on Friday morning that the project is a go. I would've mentioned it when I got here that afternoon, but we had other things that seemed more pressing." He bounced both eyebrows at her.

Taylor smiled but was thinking hard about what he'd just said. On the surface, this all sounded wonderful. Generous philanthropy—exactly the sort of thing she expected from Roman. But his larger, more public tie to Sedgefield had her concerned, particularly because of the suspected connection between the school and Little Black Book. "Are they going to name the building after you?"

He shook his head. "No. It's actually in honor of one of the history teachers at the school, Charles Braker."

Taylor breathed a small sigh of relief. At least

Roman's name wasn't going to be emblazoned across the side of the building.

"He's been retired for a while, but he was one of my favorite teachers. He made a big impact in my life. He and I actually just reconnected now that I'm sponsoring the building that will be constructed in his name."

Taylor's mind was running a million miles a minute, all because of the ties between the Baldwell School for Girls, Sedgefield Academy and every target of Little Black Book thus far. She wasn't the sort of person to be paranoid, but it worried her, especially after they'd poked around Simone Astley's house and received a threat because of it. "Does anyone know about you doing this project? Other than your old teacher or the people at the school?"

"Obviously, my office knows. They're sending out a press release about it today now that the project is a definite go. Just trying to take advantage of the situation for a little positive publicity."

Taylor reached for Roman's arm. "I think you need to stop that press release. And possibly rethink your role in this building."

"What? Why?"

Taylor looked at the time on her phone. It was nearly ten o'clock and Roman's pilot was supposed to pick him up at ten thirty. She didn't have a lot of time, so she launched right into it—her quickest explanation of the theory that Little Black Book was targeting people with ties to the two schools. When she was done, she knew what it sounded like—a wacky conspiracy theory. "The only thing I will say is that I don't give a lot of credence to these things, but Chloe and her fiancé, Parker, have spent a fair amount of time researching it, along with Chloe's mom, and they've all been targeted. Either they were threatened like we were, or in the case of Chloe's mom, she had actual posts written about her and her ex-husband."

Roman scrubbed his facial scruff with his hand. "Do you really think this could be a problem?"

"I don't want to think that, but it worries me. Yes."

"Okay. Let me call our PR office." He picked up his phone, but as soon as he looked at the screen, he was shaking his head. "It's too late. I just got an alert. It's out there in the world."

Taylor's stomach sank, but she didn't want this to ruin the end of her time with Roman. And maybe it was nothing. Maybe the tie between the two schools, an eccentric socialite who'd passed away and the anonymous social media account was all conjecture. After all, it was Chloe's mom who came up with the theory, and she was known more for a long string of marriages and some admirable charity work than her amateur sleuthing skills. "You know, hopefully this is just me worrying unnecessarily. You're doing a nice thing for your school, and if it means you're going to be in Connecticut more often, it makes me happy."

"I try not to worry about things that I can't control." He smiled and leaned in for another kiss. "And

I like making you happy, Taylor. I like knowing that I can do that."

She loved hearing him say those words. "I hope I can make you happy, too. And proud."

He narrowed his sights on her. "Proud?"

"Yes. I want the hotel to be something that you can look at and feel good about having had a role in."

"I know we've only known each other for a short time, but I'm already incredibly proud of you. You've taken your life by the horns, Taylor. Not everyone has the courage to do that."

Any vote of confidence was good, but one that came from Roman seemed like a precious gift. She would hold on to it forever. "I won't let you down."

"I know you won't."

Just then she heard the rotors, and they both looked out the kitchen window to watch as the helicopter came into view, slowly dropping down onto the grass.

"That's my ride." Roman picked up his bag.

"I'll walk you out." She opened the door to the backyard, taking his hand and ambling across the grass with him. Sadness was creeping in, but she fought it off. Roman was leaving, but he wasn't leaving *her*. They would be together again. Still, she realized that even with the support of her friends and Roman, this project she was undertaking was a solitary effort. It would be hard. It would be lonely.

"Goodbye, Taylor." Roman threaded his hands into her hair and brought her lips to his, leaving her with a kiss she might never forget. "I'll see you soon."

"Goodbye, Roman." She ducked out from under the rotor blades and ran up the slope to the pool, then turned to watch him leave, hoping "soon" could get here so much faster.

"I'm glad we had this chance to look over the project before Fiona has the baby," Roman said to Derrick as they strolled through what would eventually become the lobby of their new hotel. The windows were dingy and boarded up. The floors were dusty. But the bones here were good. And that was all that mattered.

"I'm glad we had a chance to do this, too. We're going to be at such a crucial phase with the project after the baby's born. It's going to be hard for me to get much work done the first month. This helps me feel like I have a thorough grasp of our next steps. Thanks again for getting things moving with the structural engineer."

"I don't want you to worry about it. It's not like I haven't done this before. Our project manager is top-notch and we can always do a video call with you if you aren't able to get away."

"I know. I just wanted this to be a collaboration, Roman. I want to work on it together. Not just put in some money and cash in later."

"Right." *Collaboration.* That was the word Taylor was always using, the one that he'd given her a hard time about. It had taken Derrick to tell him that not everyone approached every project or problem the way he did.

"Is everything okay? You seem distracted," Derrick said. "Which isn't like you at all. Especially when we're talking business."

Roman wandered over to the windows and looked out on the street. As enamored as he could be with the city, he really wished he could be somewhere greener. Like Connecticut. With Taylor. Yes, he'd been there hours ago. He still yearned for it. For her. "What? No. I'm just thinking."

Derrick placed his hand on Roman's shoulder. "Thinking and distraction. Same thing. What's going on?"

Roman felt more than a little foolish for what he was considering saying. He was a forty-year-old man, not a schoolboy with a crush. But the truth was that he couldn't get Taylor off his mind. She was the only place his brain wanted to go. And once he started thinking about her, he couldn't get himself to consider any other subject. "It's Taylor. I went to see her again over the weekend."

Derrick grinned and leaned against the wall, crossing his arms over his chest. "Tell me more."

Roman closed his eyes and pinched the bridge of his nose. "I don't know what to tell you. Other than that she's incredible. She has so much spirit locked up inside of her. So much life. She makes me look at the whole world in a different way." He opened his eyes and looked at his brother. "Do you have any idea how many truly uninspired people I meet? Or work with?"

Derrick arched both eyebrows at him. "I work in real estate. I think I have a pretty good idea. And frankly, I'm guessing that you probably work with a lot more creative people than I ever get to."

"You're right. I'm blowing this out of proportion. I need to stop putting her on a pedestal in my mind. She probably doesn't even want that."

Derrick reached for Roman's arm. "No. That's not what I'm saying at all. What I'm saying is that you already spend a lot of your time surrounded by pretty extraordinary people. The fact that she's standing out like this really says something, doesn't it? About just how special she is?"

Roman turned and perched on the edge of the window ledge. "I'm worried that the things I've built up in my head aren't real."

"Like what?"

"The thoughts. The words that are swimming around in there. They don't make any sense."

"You're talking in riddles."

"Am I?"

"Yes. Just spit it out. Are you in love with her?"

Thank goodness Derrick had said the word so Roman didn't have to. "That's what I'm worried about. That I'm falling."

"Falling *in love*. Say it, Roman. I promise it won't kill you."

Or would it? Roman was unconvinced that it couldn't at least hurt him. The only other time he'd fallen in love, it had ended so painfully that he'd been sure he would never recover. "I'm worried that I'm falling in love. Or more precisely, I'm worried that I've convinced myself that I'm falling in love."

"I'm not sure I understand the difference."

"I always believed that there was only one right person for everyone. One true love. And when I was with Abby, I thought that she was the only person I would ever feel that way about." He got up and wandered to the center of the room. Something about moving helped him clear his head. "And when you lose someone, then you only double down on that idea. You're so deep in grief that you tell yourself that you had your one chance at love and it's gone. And even after everything I found out about her afterward, I can still look back at moments with Abby and remember what it was like to think no one would ever match what she meant to me."

"First off, I don't think Abby was your one true love. Maybe there's more than one person for some people."

"But doesn't that feel wrong? I mean, think about the way you feel about Fiona. Can you imagine that there's another woman somewhere on the earth who you could love just as much?"

Derrick shook his head. "No. I can't imagine that. But that's what love means. You're all in on that person. And no one else matters. But it doesn't mean that life doesn't change. And love along with it. Your life changed when Abby died. And then it changed again when you met Taylor. They're two separate people and two different events. Neither one of them has to have any bearing on the other."

"But they aren't entirely unconnected. I'm the common thread."

"So all I can tell you is to listen to your gut. Which I know you're good at because you do that all day long with your work. Your instincts have served you very well, Roman. They've made you millions and millions of dollars. So I would just keep doing that. Open your heart and your mind and listen to your gut when it comes to Taylor."

Roman nodded, taking in his brother's words. This was very similar advice to what he'd told Taylor. "Okay. I can do that." His phone beeped with a text, and he fished his phone out of his pocket. He saw Taylor's name, which made his heart flutter. But then he saw the message. Call me ASAP. Little Black Book went after you. I'm so sorry.

"What is it?" Derrick asked. "Something's wrong. I can see it on your face."

"Taylor sent me something. Apparently a social media account went after me, but I don't know what that means, exactly." Before he called her, he wanted to see it for himself. He opened the app and searched for it. When he clicked on it, he told himself he was prepared for anything. It turned out he was wrong. His stomach pitched and rolled as he read the tale of a man who fell in love, lost his wife in an accident, then used the resources of his wealthy family to make it all go away.

Derrick grabbed the phone from Roman and

looked for himself, scrolling through the images Little Black Book had dug up of each Abby and Roman, including one of them together that Roman was sure had been destroyed. There were even photos of the accident scene. Roman had never laid eyes on that one—the police had been sure he'd be too upset. "Oh, my God. Roman. How did anyone find out about this?"

Roman's head was spinning so fast it felt like someone had just punched him. Visions of his past were flashing before his eyes, and not just because they'd been displayed for all the world to see in a social media post. "I…uh…I don't know." But of course, his brain arrived at one conclusion very quickly, an answer that he did not want to be true. Taylor knew about the events that were in those pictures. She was one of the only people who knew. And she'd warned him this might happen. "But I think Taylor might know."

Just then his phone rang. Derrick still had it in his hand. "It's Taylor, Roman."

"I…" He was struggling to keep it together, doing everything in his power to think straight. "I don't think I can talk to her."

Derrick clamped a hand on Roman's shoulder. "No. You need to. If you think she might know how this happened, you should find out so we can make it go away." He caught Roman's attention with a plaintive stare. "But more than anything, I think you love her. And this is what love is about. Being there for someone when everything falls apart. Let her be there for you."

The notion of it was completely counterintuitive. Here he was being consumed by worries that the woman he was falling for was somehow involved in this horrific event that was only a few minutes old. He was supposed to talk to her about it? Now?

The phone continued to ring.

"I'm answering it," Derrick said. "You're going to ruin your life if this call goes to voice mail."

That snapped Roman back into the moment. "No. I'll take it." He snatched the phone back from his brother. "Taylor?"

"Oh, thank God. Roman. I was so worried you weren't going to answer." The sound of Taylor's voice buoyed him in a way he had not expected. It started to lift the fog in his mind. "I am so sorry this happened. We have to find out who did it. Remember when you asked if someone was spying on us at the house? I'm worried that you might be right."

It felt like the breath had been sucked right out of him. Just as quickly as his mind had gone to a dark place where she might have been involved in this terrible thing that had happened to him, it was switched to a completely different mindset—one that was worried only about her. He knew she couldn't be involved. He was certain. "You can't be there, Taylor. You have to get out. Now."

"I'm already packing up the car. I'm going to push back my contractor meetings. And I'm going to call Bruce to let him know what's going on."

That was when it hit Roman. "Taylor, no. Don't call Bruce."

"What? Why?"

"What if he's behind this?"

The other end of the line went eerily quiet. "Oh, my God. I have to call my dad. Right away."

"I want you to call him from the car, but don't take the Porsche. Remember when you were surprised Bruce had washed it? That worries me." He was impressed that he was able to think at such a high level right now.

"Oh, wow. Okay."

"Or I can send the helicopter for you."

"No. Roman. I'd rather make my exit a quiet one if that's okay with you."

"Yes. That's smart. Where are you going to go?"

"I'll come back to the city. I guess I'll drop my stuff at my apartment, then I'd like to see you. I need to lay eyes on you. I need to know that you're okay. I'm so sorry this happened. I'm sure you're in shock."

Funny, but he had been five minutes ago. Now that he was in crisis mode, he felt like he could deal with anything. It had always been the quieter moments in life that got to him. "Call me when you get here. Maybe I can come over. Or you can come to my place."

"Yeah, sure. Whatever works. I still need to grab a few more things and lock up the house. It might be a couple of hours, depending on traffic."

Derrick's phone rang and Roman saw him answer it out of the corner of his eye. "Be safe, Taylor." *Please get to me okay. I need to see you. I need to tell you things.*

"I will. I'll see you soon."

"Bye." Roman hung up the phone at the exact moment Derrick ended his own call. "Taylor's on her way to the city."

"Okay. Well, in case you were wondering if today could get any crazier, that was Fiona. She thinks she's in labor. Contractions are regular and they're getting closer together. I told her to get in a cab and go straight to the hospital. I'm going to meet her there. But I need you to go to my house and babysit Polly because the nanny is sick. Fiona's going to leave her with our downstairs neighbor for the time being."

What was that expression about raining and pouring? Roman, Derrick, Taylor and Fiona were living it right now. "Yes. Of course. Whatever you need. Let's get out of here."

Eleven

Taylor left the Porsche behind and instead took the white Range Rover her mom used when she was at the estate. She called her dad from the car before she'd even pulled out of the garage.

"Hi, honey. How are you?" He was always sunny and upbeat with Taylor, making the prospect of telling him what was going on that much more difficult.

"I'm okay. But I need to talk to you if you can spare a few minutes."

"Anything for you. Are you at the summer house?"

"I'm leaving, actually."

"Taylor. You're leaving? Don't you have contractor appointments set up this week? You aren't running away from your problems, are you? We've talked about this. Sometimes work is hard and you just have to get through it."

She hadn't thought about the fact that her dad might see it that way. "I'm not running away. If anything, I'm trying to save my entire future. My career and my love life."

"Sounds serious."

"It is." Taylor launched into everything—Bruce, Little Black Book and the story about Roman that had shown up on the social media account. When she was finished telling the story, she knew exactly how absurd it sounded, but this was the state of things. If she hadn't experienced these events firsthand, she might be inclined to think they weren't true. "That's the abbreviated version."

"It sounds to me like I need to talk to Bruce."

"I'm worried that he's just going to take off, Dad. Or deflect and lie to you. If he's involved, we need to know who he is or who he's working for. I'm afraid we'll never know that if you confront him with zero evidence."

"So I need to get someone to the house and make sure everything is secure. But without arousing any suspicion."

"Exactly." An idea popped into Taylor's head. "Dad, do you trust the guy at Morton's Construction? You know him, right?"

"Absolutely. I've known Billy for years. He's done a fair amount of work at the house."

"Perfect. I have an appointment with him this afternoon that I was going to postpone. But maybe he can be our cover. Or maybe he can help."

"I'll call him right away. As soon as we get off the phone. I'm sure we can work something out."

Taylor felt as though she could breathe at least a small sigh of relief. "Thank you, Dad. I swear this isn't another one of my panic situations. Things with the estate are going great. This is just an extremely strange bump in the road. Certainly one I never saw coming."

"Life is like that sometimes, honey. You just have to get through it. It sounds to me like you're doing everything right."

"Thank you. We'll see how it all pans out."

"Can we talk about Roman Scott? Or is that getting too personal?"

Taylor wasn't surprised her dad had picked up on that—she'd been the one who'd just said that she was saving her career and her love life. She hadn't gone into detail about their relationship before, but she'd definitely mentioned him. And she'd raved about him, at least a little bit. It would have been so easy to brush it aside and tell her dad that it was nothing. Or keep him in the dark about it. That was the easy way out. No father wanted to know the details of their daughter's love life, especially if it wasn't a permanent thing. But Taylor had this feeling that there was so much more with Roman. And she had to keep going with her gut. She couldn't stop now.

"We're involved, Dad. I care about him a lot. So much."

"I see. He's not another guy who's just going to break your heart, is he?"

Taylor hoped that the way she felt wouldn't ultimately prove to be hopelessly naive. "I can't see that happening. No."

"Do you love him?"

The first word that popped into her head was *yes*. But something told her that when and if she ever owned up to it, Roman deserved to be the first to know. "I'm not quite there yet, but it's pointing in that direction."

"All your mom and I want is for you to be happy."

"Well, he makes me happy."

"Then that's perfect as far as I'm concerned."

"Will you call me and let me know what happens with the house and Bruce?"

"Absolutely. Don't worry about it. I will take care of this part. You get to the city, where I know you can be safe."

"Thanks, Dad. I love you."

"I love you, too, honey."

She ended the call and focused on her breathing as she drove. After her chat with her dad, it was hard not to think about how she would have dealt with this a year or two ago. He wasn't being cruel when he asked if she was running from her life. She'd done that more than once—moved on to greener pastures when things got tough. Yes, she'd been through the wringer. But she'd put herself through it as well. But she felt as though she'd learned to move beyond her mistakes.

A text from Roman came through, which showed up on the large monitor on Taylor's dashboard. Change of plans. Fiona is in labor. Can you meet me at their house?

Oh, wow. Another complication. This day was one for the record books. "Text Roman Scott," Taylor said aloud.

A tone beeped. "What is your message for Roman Scott?" her phone asked.

"Of course. Send me the address. I'll get there as soon as I can."

"Ready to send?" her phone asked.

"Yes."

Taylor drew in a deep breath and braced herself for what was next, whatever that might be. And as she got closer and closer to Roman with every passing mile, she hoped like hell that her gut was speaking the truth to her when it came to him. She hoped that this time, her running to a man would turn out better than every time one had run away from her.

"Uncle Roman, you aren't coloring with me." His niece, Polly, had a few hundred pieces of paper spread across the kitchen table, along with dozens of markers and crayons.

"I'm sorry, sweetheart. I'm distracted." That was an understatement. Between Derrick taking Fiona to the hospital, Roman setting up shop at his brother and sister-in-law's apartment so he could babysit Polly and waiting for Taylor to arrive, he had his hands full.

"That's what Daddy always says when he's busy with work."

Roman drew in a deep breath and put his arm around her, then kissed her on top of her head. "I'm sorry. Now, what are we drawing?"

"Princesses, with castles and horses and unicorns."

Roman glanced at Polly's drawing, which did indeed contain all of those elements. He wasn't sure he could keep up with her artistic talents, but he was going to try. "Got it." He didn't get very far when he received a text from Derrick. Baby is here. A girl. She and Fiona are doing great. More soon.

Roman quickly tapped out a reply. Congratulations! Should I tell Polly?

Let's wait. Tell her that Fiona and I will do a video call in a few hours.

Will do. Roman set aside his phone, ecstatic for his brother and sister-in-law, and oddly relieved that this day had been completely turned on its head. If Fiona hadn't gone into labor, he would be sitting in his office right now, stewing over the social media brouhaha that had been unleashed. The arrival of his niece and his worries over Taylor's safety up at the house in Connecticut had put everything into perspective, and it had done it like the flick of a switch. He'd spent more than a decade building a reputation. If the airing of his tragic past was meant to hurt him, he wasn't going to allow it. He'd lived that pain. And he didn't much care about anyone's opinion of the events that had happened. It didn't mean that he was happy it had happened—quite the contrary. But he wasn't going to stress about it when there were other more important things going on. "That was your dad texting me," he said to Polly. "He says that your mom is doing great, and they will do a video call with you in a little bit."

"Okay." Polly seemed unconcerned with whether or not her sibling had arrived.

Roman's phone went off again. This time, it was from Taylor. I'm downstairs. Do you want to buzz me up?

Yes. Two secs. He got up from the table and rushed to the intercom, where he pressed the button to allow Taylor access to the building. He unlocked the front door and stood on the landing, waiting for her to come up. The minute he saw her, his handle on his stress level disappeared. What if she didn't feel the same way he felt? What if she was going to tell him that he was moving far too fast? Those were real possibilities, and if either of those things came to pass, he might not be so able to brush off the Little Black Book story.

"How are you?" she asked when she reached the landing.

"I'm fine. Please. Come on in." He followed her inside the house and closed the door behind them, then immediately took her hand, but she apparently wanted more. She pulled him into a tight embrace. As he returned the hug, his doubts began to fade. He closed his eyes, soaking up the sensation of having her in his arms. This felt right. He wasn't sure how Taylor had worked her way into his head and heart so quickly, but she had.

"Are you sure you're okay?" she asked. "I feel terrible about what happened. I can't figure out if I feel worse for warning you or if that should make me feel better."

"I think it probably took the edge off a little bit. As shocked as I was when it happened, you'd laid the foundation in my brain. It didn't come completely out of left field."

She managed half a smile and took his hand, playing with his fingers. "You know, you had every reason to suspect I had some role in it. And you didn't do that. At all. I'm not sure I would have been so charitable if I was in your position."

He sighed. "You know, it was this very fleeting thought. I won't lie about that. But the second I heard your voice, I knew that there was no way you would do that to me. And something kicked in and told me that your safety was a much bigger concern. You became my real worry."

Her smile grew and she stepped closer to him. "It makes me really happy to hear that."

"Good." He kissed her softly, wishing they could be alone.

"Uncle Roman," Polly's little voice came from behind him.

He abruptly turned, feeling a bit embarrassed, like a teenager that had been caught making out when they shouldn't be. "Polly. I'm sorry. I want you to meet my friend Taylor."

"Hello, Polly." Taylor crouched down in front of her.

Polly made a careful appraisal of Taylor. "Are you my uncle's girlfriend? I saw you kissing him."

Taylor peered up at Roman and grinned. "I think so?"

Roman wanted to put a quick end to any uncertainty on that topic. "Yes, Polly. Taylor is my girlfriend."

"Okay," Polly said. "I'm going to go color some more." She turned and flitted off for the kitchen.

"I hope you're okay with coloring. Polly picks the subject matter. There's not a lot of artistic license to be taken," Roman said.

"Oh, I was a very bossy little girl, too. I'm sure Polly and I will get along just great." Taylor followed behind Polly, and Roman trailed behind her.

Taylor took a seat with Polly, and his niece explained the rules of what they would be working on while Roman fetched Taylor an ice-cold glass of water. He joined them, sitting right next to Taylor. And as the three of them chatted about things like Polly's preschool and whether or not she was excited about being a big sister, Roman felt like his entire future was opening up. Life was moving forward. There was no more need to look back. He'd long taken that approach, but today was the first day when he truly felt it. Down to his bones.

After a half hour or so, Derrick placed the video

call he'd promised. Roman answered and let Polly climb up into his lap so she could see her new baby sister.

"Polly, look," Fiona said, looking tired but glowing as she held the baby so Derrick could capture the moment with his phone. "It's your new baby sister."

Polly got impossibly close to the screen, nearly rubbing her nose against it. "What's her name?" she asked.

"We aren't sure yet, honey. We're trying to decide between Avery and Charlotte. What do you think?"

"Avery." Polly was very quick with her answer.

Derrick and Fiona looked at each other and smiled, then Fiona shrugged. "Okay, then. Avery it is."

Polly clapped her hands furiously. "When are you coming home?"

"Mommy and Avery have to stay one night, but I'll be home in a few hours," Derrick said. "Is everything okay there?"

"Yes," Polly answered. "Uncle Roman's girlfriend, Taylor, came over. She's really nice and much better at coloring than Uncle Roman."

Roman laughed and glanced at Taylor, whose expression was a perfect mix of polite embarrassment and happiness.

Derrick grinned from ear to ear. "Okay, honey. Let me talk to your uncle, okay?"

"Okay, Daddy." Polly jumped off Roman's lap and returned to monopolizing Taylor's attention.

Roman got up from the table and wandered over

to the sliding doors that led to the terrace. "Everything okay there?"

"Yeah. We're good. The baby's already nursing like a champ. Fiona is well. All in all, I'm feeling like a very lucky man today."

Funny, but Roman was feeling the same way. Even when plenty had gone wrong. None of it seemed to matter anymore. "Congratulations. I'm so happy for you. I can't wait to meet Avery." His voice cracked at the end there, thinking about this love for his brother and how he would not be the man he was today without him.

"I can't wait to meet Taylor. I only got a fleeting glance of her that night at the auction."

Roman turned and watched her with Polly. His heart flipped in the center of his chest. "I'm looking forward to that, too." He said his goodbye to his brother, then ended the call and strode back to Taylor and Polly. "We probably need to think about dinner soon. What if we go supereasy and order a pizza? I don't think any of us feel like cooking."

"I think that sounds like an excellent idea," Taylor said.

Roman took charge of the situation, placing an order, then running down the street to pick it up when it was ready. When he returned to the house, Taylor and Polly had set the outdoor dining table. Taylor had taken some initiative and opened a bottle of red wine. The three sat and ate, laughing at a few points more than was probably reasonable. It was the most fun Roman could remember having in a long time. All he could think was that he wanted more of this. And it was only going to work with Taylor.

After dinner, Polly and Taylor read books on the couch until Derrick got home. Roman gave his brother a huge hug when he came through the door, then walked him into the room. Polly practically flew off the sofa. "Daddy!"

"Hey, baby girl." Derrick crouched down and wrapped her up in his arms.

"Derrick, I want you to meet Taylor," Roman said, just as she got up and joined him.

"It's really nice to meet you, Taylor. I've heard so much about you." Derrick wasn't super sly about it when he grinned at her, then looked at Roman and delivered a look that essentially said, *Don't you dare mess this up.*

"It's wonderful to meet you, too. I've had the best time with Polly. And thank you for letting me hang out at your house while Roman was watching her. I feel a bit like I've intruded on your very special day."

Derrick shook his head. "Are you kidding me? Do you know how long I've waited for my brother to meet someone like you?"

Taylor looked down at the floor for a moment. "A long time?"

"Too long," Roman answered for his brother.

"I'm going to go tuck Polly in. Then I'm going to pass out. I'm exhausted," Derrick said. "But, Taylor, it was really, really nice to meet you. Next time we see you, we'll try to make it a more normal visit, meaning Fiona will actually be here and not in the hospital. You guys are welcome to stay as long as you want."

"We've got half a bottle of wine to finish," Roman said. "So I think we'll drink it out on the terrace then get out of your hair."

"Lock up when you leave," Derrick said as he carried Polly down the hall.

Roman and Taylor sauntered out to the terrace, hand in hand. It was the most glorious early-summer evening, with a soft breeze. He filled their glasses, and they stood at the glass railing where they could get the best view of Central Park.

"I meant what I said when I told Derrick that I feel like an intruder today. But thank you for including me," Taylor said. "It means a lot."

"It's the only way that today could have happened, Taylor. It's the only thing that would have made sense."

"It could have gone a million different ways, Roman. You could have not taken my phone call earlier. You could have blamed me for what happened with Little Black Book. And I would have had zero reason to be upset with you for either of those things."

"I don't think either of those reactions would have made sense to me."

"Are you saying you were following your gut?"

He grinned. "I told you to follow your instincts, but I also told myself that I need to take my own advice. Otherwise, I'm going to have zero chance at happiness." He looked back at the house for a moment, thinking about the life his brother had built for himself and how badly Roman realized he wanted that, too. And the only thing that made sense right now was to chase that sliver of happiness with Taylor. His pulse was pounding in his ears as everything he wanted to say to her was competing for a chance to spill from his mouth. He wasn't sure where to start, so he went with the most direct approach, starting by turning back to her and taking her hand. "I love you, Taylor. I know that sounds impossible. Unrealistic. Irrational. I realize that we haven't known each other very long, but I'm hoping that you will make room for me in your life. Because I've already made room for you in my heart."

Taylor stood frozen for a moment, and he felt as though his breaths were frozen in the center of his chest. She was that beautiful and wonderful and it was going to hurt so much if she didn't feel the same way about him. "Roman, I love you, too. I do."

And just like that, his breath broke free, and he was filled with life and light and hope. He pulled her into his arms and kissed her quickly, but only so he could make sure this was all real. "Really?"

"Really. I started falling for you the minute you pushed me into the back of your limo."

"That can't be true. We hardly knew each other then."

"You talked about instincts, but you also talked about following your heart. And my heart was telling me from the very beginning that you were right for me. I think that's what made me break my promise to myself to not get involved. To break it again and again."

Roman smiled and kissed her again, much more slowly this time. "You've made me so happy, Taylor. I'm not sure if you appreciate that."

"Oh, no. I do appreciate it. Because you've made me just as happy." She smiled wide at him and their gazes connected. "I don't think I've ever been as happy as I am now."

He felt the zap of attraction he'd endured the first time he laid eyes on her, only it was so much stronger now. "Now what?"

"We get out of here and go to your place or mine and take off our clothes and have superhot sex?"

"Which one is closer?" he asked.

"Your place."

"I think we have our answer, then." He laughed again and drew a finger under her chin. "Although, I was talking a little more big picture than sex, Taylor. As appealing as it all sounds."

"What did you have in mind, Roman?"

"A collaboration."

She cocked her head to one side and narrowed her gaze on him. "I thought you were opposed to that."

"Not with you."

Twelve

"How many bugs did they find?" Roman asked when he and Taylor arrived back at her family's Connecticut estate. She'd stayed away for ten days, enough time for Roman and Taylor to spend a nice stretch of time together in the city, and for Taylor's father to hire a security team to do a thorough sweep of the house. That was when the source of the leaks to Little Black Book was discovered.

"Eleven recording devices. Nine in the house, including one in the study where I like to hang out the most. The one we were sitting in the night you told me everything. And there were another two in the cars we use the most, including my Porsche, just like you suspected."

"And cameras?"

"Not as many of those. Only three. One in here." She looked around the kitchen. "One in the front hall and one outside the front door—I guess so they could watch people coming and going? They probably didn't count on anyone arriving by helicopter."

"So, nothing by the pool?"

Taylor laughed. She shared his worry about that exact same thing. "No, you naughty boy. Nothing by the pool."

"Phew. That's a big relief." He took Taylor's hand and pulled it to his lips, kissing her fingers. "It's unbelievable. I've dealt with corporate espionage before, but never anything like this."

"Believe me, my dad was shocked when he got the full report. The local police brought Bruce in for questioning and he confessed to the whole thing. But he was taking orders from someone else, and he doesn't know who it was. He basically took the money and the assignment."

"Poor guy. Some people will do anything for money."

Taylor shrugged. "I'd like to think that isn't true, but maybe it is."

"Should we go drop our bags upstairs? When are your friends set to arrive?"

She glanced at the time on her phone. It was a little after four. "They should be here in a half hour." Parker and Chloe were coming up under the auspices of discussing the wedding, but Taylor had a feeling that Little Black Book was going to be a big topic of conversation. Parker was not only dead set on taking down the social media account, he was hoping he could pull Roman in on the effort. Or at least that was what Chloe had said. Taylor wasn't necessarily opposed to the idea, but she did want to keep moving forward. The last ten days with Roman had been absolutely magical. She was going to do everything she could to keep their relationship going. That meant that she was focused on the road ahead of her, with Roman at the very top of the list. He was all that mattered.

Taylor and Roman made their way upstairs, and she realized when they reached the second floor that the only obvious place for them to go was to her room. Yes, that was where he'd slept for part of his first visit to the house, and for all of his second, but this was the first time that they'd arrived together. It was both wonderful and a little nerve-racking to know that their couple-hood was so settled that neither had to ask the question. How did she feel more comfortable with Roman after only a few weeks than she'd ever felt with other men over longer periods of time? *It's true love*, had been Alex's answer when Taylor had posed the question. Taylor hoped that was true. She not only couldn't envision a future without Roman in it, she didn't want to. He was her everything.

"I can clean out part of the closet for you," Taylor offered when they arrived in her room. "To give you some room for your clothes. I know you're only staying for the weekend, but you'll be going back and forth. So you might as well have a space to leave some of your belongings."

"That would be great. Thanks."

Taylor cleared off one closet rod and a shelf, then emptied a dresser drawer. "Just let me know if you need anything else."

He nodded. "This is plenty for me."

Taylor couldn't help but notice that he wasn't actually unpacking. "Is everything okay?"

"Couldn't be better."

Maybe he needed some time to settle in. "Okay. I'm going to put away my toiletries and make some space for you in the bathroom."

"That would be perfect. Thank you."

Taylor did exactly that, then returned to the closet. She noticed that Roman was being very careful putting away his things. "Are you sure everything is okay?"

He nodded. "Yep. If you want to go downstairs, I'll meet you there in a few."

She took that to mean Roman needed some privacy. She wasn't about to deny him that, so she did exactly as he suggested. "Okey doke. I'll open a bottle of wine."

A few minutes after she arrived in the kitchen, the doorbell rang. She rushed down the hall and flung it open, so happy to see Chloe and Parker. Even better, Roman was making his way down the stairs. Taylor hugged her friends, then made the introductions.

"Roman, I've really been looking forward to

meeting you," Chloe said. "Taylor told me just enough about you to make me intensely curious."

Roman shot Taylor an inquisitive look that was inexplicably hot and flirtatious. "I'll have to ask her later exactly what she said."

"And maybe I'll tell you or maybe I won't," Taylor said. "Let's go sit out by the pool. Our new caretaker left a charcuterie platter in the fridge. We'll open some wine."

"Sounds like a plan to me," Parker said.

The four got settled out on the terrace, exactly where Taylor had sat with Chloe and Alex a few short weeks ago. Roman poured the wine and Parker dug into the food.

"Taylor, I cannot believe that your caretaker was involved with Little Black Book. That's so incredible. And scary," Parker said.

"I'm telling you, there's something to this whole Baldwell School and Sedgefield Academy connection," Taylor said. "Roman was targeted the same day his company announced they were partnering with Sedgefield to construct a new building on campus."

"The whole thing is one big puzzle," Parker said. "And I really hope I can figure it out."

"It's all he talks about," Chloe said. "He's got folders on the topic."

"Maybe you need to come up here early for the wedding," Roman said. "So we can sit down and look at everything."

Parker planted an elbow on the table and pointed at Roman. "Yes. I like the way you think."

"I was sort of hoping we could take a break from Little Black Book during our wedding," Chloe said.

"Yeah. Of course. But this would be before the wedding, right?" Parker asked, which made Chloe roll her eyes.

"Are you guys still sure you want to have it here?" Taylor took a sip of her wine. "I mean, my dad had the entire property swept, but there's only so much privacy we can promise you. If someone wanted to fly a drone over the house during your ceremony, we can't really stop them."

"No. We really want to have the ceremony here. It's our best chance to have a small wedding and have it done quickly. Parker and I don't want to wait to start our lives together." Chloe leaned over the arm of her chair and gave him a kiss.

It made Taylor immensely happy to see her friend so in love, but it made it that much better knowing that she, too, was head over heels. As if Roman sensed what she was thinking, he reached for her hand and gave it a tiny squeeze. "Perfect. Then we can work out some of the final details while you guys are here this weekend."

"I'm happy to help," Roman said. "With whatever needs to be done, especially around the house. Painting. Maintenance. Whatever you need."

"You know I have a contractor to help with all of that. Plus, how are you possibly going to have time?" Taylor asked.

"I'll make time. I'm hoping to be here a lot. If that's okay with you."

Taylor was taken aback by that. Roman was so tied to his business, and he hadn't brought it up at all, which Taylor had assumed meant that he was going to march ahead exactly as he had before. "Really?"

He nodded. "Yep. I can work from here as long as you'll have me, and I can bop back into the city for a day when I need to. Plus, I'll need to make the occasional trip to Sedgefield while we work on construction there."

She smiled so wide her cheeks hurt. It meant so much to her that he hadn't asked her to consider setting aside her professional aspirations. He'd simply molded his own responsibilities to suit hers. "I think that sounds wonderful." She found herself drifting closer to Roman and giving him a soft and superhot kiss that was purposely laden with innuendo. She wanted him. He was making everything so damn amazing.

Parker cleared his throat. "Can I do anything to help with dinner?"

Chloe smacked his arm with the back of her hand. "Let them be in love, okay?" She turned to Taylor and smiled wide. "I love seeing you two so happy."

"Right back at ya," Taylor said. "Come on. You can help me." She and Taylor made their way into the kitchen, but there wasn't too much work to do. The caretaker had brought in some chicken Parmesan that simply needed to be heated up in the oven, along with the fixings for a salad.

"I mean what I said out there," Chloe said. "It makes me so happy to see you happy."

"I really wondered if it was ever going to happen for me."

"I didn't worry about that at all. I always knew it was simply a matter of finding a man who was just as awesome as you are."

"Thanks, Chloe. I can't wait to have your wedding here. It's going to be so much fun."

Once the salad was prepared and the chicken was hot, the four of them shared their meal out on the patio, laughing and talking for hours. The wine flowed freely, and Taylor couldn't remember a time when she'd ever felt happier. She would have wished for the night to go on forever if she wasn't also so eager to get Roman upstairs and into her bed.

"I'm wiped out," Taylor said after they'd cleaned up the dishes.

"Us, too," Chloe countered. "We'll go ahead and head up. See you in the morning."

"Yes. See you then."

Taylor and Roman tended to a few more things in the kitchen, then hand in hand walked upstairs and into her room, her heart feeling as full and light as it had ever felt. She loved having her friends here. Even better, she loved having Roman by her side.

Roman came to a stop once they crossed the threshold. He closed the door. "Taylor, I want to give you something."

"What is it? Is it you?" She tugged on his shirt and delivered a big kiss.

He laughed. "In a minute, it will be. Until then, sit on the bed and I'll bring it to you."

She padded over and perched on the edge of the mattress, doing her best to look seductive. "All I really want is you, okay?"

"You are amazing. And also impatient. One minute." He disappeared into the closet.

Taylor leaned back on her arm, realizing that this was perhaps the reason he'd been acting so strangely earlier. She and Roman hadn't exchanged any tokens of appreciation before now. It hadn't really seemed necessary. So she couldn't imagine what it could possibly be. With a guy like Roman, who had unlimited resources, it could be anything.

When he emerged from the closet, he frankly looked a bit pale. Like he might be sick. Which did not bode well for Taylor's romantic plans. "Roman, are you sure you're okay?"

He nodded eagerly, holding his hands behind his back. "Yes. I just need to give this to you and then I will feel one million times better." He took a seat next to her and placed whatever had been behind his back next to him.

Taylor didn't want to ruin the surprise, so she didn't look. He was clearly nervous about this.

He pulled her hand into his lap and looked into her eyes with the most sincere expression she'd ever seen on any man's face. She still found it funny that people thought of Roman as being gruff or distant. To her, he almost always wore his heart on his sleeve. And right now, it felt as though she held it in her hands. She hoped he knew that she would always take care of it. Always care for him. "You know, one thing that I kept thinking about at dinner was that the story coming out with Little Black Book wasn't a bad thing. Even though Parker wants them stopped and I have to agree that it should happen, for me, that whole incident was oddly wonderful. Because it was a piece of the puzzle that made me realize how much you mean to me. And that I'd spent the last decade or more in a holding pattern. With my business chugging ahead and my life on pause."

"That's such a nice way to look at it. Not every bad thing is purely bad. There's always something good to take out of any situation."

"Exactly." He drew in a deep breath. "So, I don't know if you know about internet sleuthing."

Now Taylor *really* didn't know where Roman was going with this. "You mean people who solve real-life mysteries they find online?"

"Yes. Exactly. And that's where my run-in with Little Black Book comes into play. I received an email a few days ago from a man who used to run a pawn shop up in Boston. He saw the post about Abby. And he recognized her as someone who used to come into his store all the time to sell things. He said that he developed a good nose for people who were pawning things they shouldn't, and that he would often set those items aside and not offer them for sale in the shop. He held on to one thing that Abby sold him. And once we spoke and I identified the item, he sent it to me. It came in the mail yesterday, but I wanted to wait until today to give it to you. When we could be up here and in this house."

"Why here?"

"Because this is where we fell in love."

Taylor felt her eyes welling up with moisture. This house meant so much to her, and now there was a whole new layer of meaning. "That is so sweet. Truly."

He turned and plucked the item from the bed and handed it to her. It was a small black velvet box. A jewelry box, but not a fancy one. "Open it."

Taylor's hand was trembling as she flipped open the lid. And when she saw what was inside, her breath caught in her throat. It was a simple gold ring with a pale blue stone in the center, and smaller diamonds on either side. "Sapphire?"

"Yes."

"Is this your grandmother's ring? The one you thought was gone forever?"

"It is."

Goose bumps raced along her arms. She was so overwhelmed, she wasn't sure what to say. This was such a consequential piece of Roman's history. "Are you asking me to marry you?"

"Not unless you want me to. Because if you want me to, then I'm getting down on one knee right now."

A breathy laugh left her lips. She did love that she and Roman could be very real with each other. "I would love to marry you, Roman, but it would be nice to simply spend some time as boyfriend and girlfriend, you know?"

"I get that. I do. But I still want you to have this ring because of what it represents. I thought my chance at love was gone forever. That it would never happen for me. And you not only showed me that it was possible, Taylor, you loved me in return."

"Roman, that's so sweet…"

"Hold on. There's more." He held up a finger. "You had every reason in the world to not want to love me. Every jerky guy who came before me was another reason. And you'd been hurt. But just like me, you decided to try to find a way to move past all of that." He took the ring out of the box and slipped it onto her finger. "So this is an engagement ring whenever you want it to be. And until then, this is your reminder, day by day and minute by minute, that every bad thing that happened to either of us was only paving the way for this one very good thing. For you and me to find each other."

Taylor admired the ring as it glinted in the light. She'd thought her heart couldn't possibly feel more full, and yet it had grown to twice its size. "This means the world to me. I feel like I should have given you something in return."

"Well, there are ways to show your appreciation…"

Taylor laughed and pushed him back on the bed. She hovered over him, her hands planted on either side of his head. "Hold on. I'm about to appreciate you all night long."

* * * * *

Don't miss other exciting romances by Karen Booth:

The Problem with Playboys
Best Laid Wedding Plans
Blue Collar Billionaire
All He Wants for Christmas
High Society Secrets
Once Forbidden, Twice Tempted

Available from Harlequin Desire!